RENUKA

Other books by Stephen Alter

Neglected Lives

Silk and Steel

The Godchild

RENUKA

STEPHEN ALTER

ANDRE DEUTSCH

Most of this novel was written while I was Writer-in-Residence at the Institute of Culture and Communication at the East–West Center in Honolulu, Hawaii. S.A.

First published 1989 by
André Deutsch Limited
105–106 Great Russell Street, London WC1B 3LJ
Copyright © 1989 by Stephen Alter

ISBN 0 233 98374 0

Printed and bound in Great Britain by
WBC Bristol and Maesteg

For Diana Athill

CHAPTER 1

Each of these is a poem; that's how I look at them.

CURRIED MEAT LOAF   **Lois Keck**

1 pound minced lean mutton	1/2 cup yoghurt (dehi)
1 cup grated turnips	2 teaspoons salt
2 eggs, slightly beaten	1/2 teaspoon pepper
1/4 cup grated onions	1/2 teaspoon ginger
2 large cloves garlic	2 teaspoons curry powder

Blend all the ingredients together. Pack lightly into loaf pan. Bake in hot oven (400 degrees) about 1 hour. Turn out on serving platter. Garnish with fresh coriander. Serves six.

Lois Keck stays at Sylvan Lodge. Her husband is a dentist and works somewhere in Maharashtra. They're Mennonites and Lois always wears her hair in a bun, covered by one of those lace doilies. She's a stern, uncompromising woman. Her children have all grown up and gone back to the States but she keeps coming to the hillside each summer. We always say hello whenever we pass each other on the path but that's as far as either of us will go. It's not just that Lois is older than me but there's a difference of opinion in her eyes. I can always see it, a hesitant look of disapproval and then that cold, stern smile. Dr Keck comes up for a couple of weeks in July. He is more friendly than his wife and bows his shoulders when he greets me. One day I saw them walking through the rain, sharing an umbrella and for the first time I thought that once upon a time they might have loved each other.

The Kecks have four children, all of whom have graduated. I think there were three boys and a girl, polite and blond, ordinary sort of kids, thin and rangy like their father. It's no wonder really, if Lois expects to feed six people with that meat loaf. My two boys would finish it off by themselves, though the turnips might slow them down. Maybe that's her secret.

Lois only gave me one recipe. She had written it out carefully in her meticulous handwriting and took a moment finding it in her purse, when she stopped me after church. I had passed out index cards to everybody in the Women's Club and left a stack at the Community Centre for anyone who wanted more. That makes it easier, so that I can sort and file them. Otherwise everyone would be giving me scraps of paper with recipes scribbled back and front, and afterwards, when someone doesn't get their name into the cookbook, they're all upset and claim they gave you theirs and how much better it would have been than someone else's. It's hard to believe how touchy some women can get when it comes to recipes.

Lois was wearing a simple, shapeless dress, patterned with grey flowers. Her purse was a black, old-fashioned, patent leather handbag with a metal clasp. I always think of her as a spinster and it's hard to believe she has a husband and a family. She finally found the recipe card and gave it to me, a little flustered and impatient from her search. I thanked her very much and went to find the boys. They always start climbing trees in their Sunday clothes.

Later, when I read the recipe, I thought of Lois and tried to picture her making the meat loaf for her kids. These really are like poems. I can tell so many things about a woman from her recipes, even if I don't know her very well. The way she writes it down, the ingredients, the instructions, the measurements and temperatures. Each has its meaning and significance.

'What's for supper?' They always ask.

'Meat loaf,' I said. 'It's a new recipe from Mrs Keck.'

'But a meat loaf's a meat loaf isn't it?' said Michael. 'They're all the same.'

'Not this one,' I said. 'It's special.'

'Special,' said Tim, 'how come? What's in it?'

'Wait and see,' I said.

'Mom, you're always trying out these new kinds of things. Why can't we just eat normal food?'

'Yeah, remember Mrs Porter's cornflake casserole.' Tim made a face.

'You just have to put up with a few disasters,' I said.

'Even Tick wouldn't eat that casserole.'

Tick is our dog, a golden retriever with the appetite of a goat and the temperament of a hibernating teddy bear.

Dear Frank,

I didn't realize how long it's been since my last letter. Four whole weeks! There are so many things happening with this cookbook, meetings almost every day; I hardly get a chance to breath. The boys both wrote last Sunday and I hope that will make up for me not writing. I know how lonely it gets down there and you always write such good letters. Mine are usually scattered, hurried notes. Sometimes I feel I shouldn't have taken on this job as editor, it's more than I really bargained for.

Tonight I made one of the recipes I'm trying out, a meat loaf by Lois Keck. The boys turned up their noses at first

3

but Tim actually asked for seconds in the end. Poor guys, they don't really like the idea of being used as guinea pigs for all these recipes. Both of them have grown up so quickly it's hard to believe. I wish that you could have more time with them before they leave us. I know that's stupid of me but it seems unfair that we should have to live apart. Of course, there isn't any choice, but sometimes I wish we could be a family for once, not just during the holidays but for a year or two.

The monsoons are in full swing. We had our first real downpour last weekend and since then there's been a lot of mist and rain. We had so many leaks I ran out of pots and pans to put under the drips. There was a huge drip right in the middle of the bedroom. Tim and Michael had to help me move the bed aside. There's already a big damp patch on the dining room ceiling. I don't know why these roofs just can't be sealed. The chowkidar went up with a bucket of tar and I tried to show him all the places where it was leaking. He spent about three hours on the roof and it's a little better now, though the dining room is still pretty bad.

There's been a major landslide on the motor road and the traffic was cut off for almost two days. Taxis and other cars are getting through but it still hasn't been cleared for buses. Everything seems to fall apart at this time of year. We had no electricity for three nights in a row and even tonight the voltage keeps fluctuating. Tim and Michael have been doing their homework by candlelight. The worst part of it is that because of the voltage fluctuations one of the pumps down in the valley burned out and there hasn't been any water for the last two days. It's so frustrating to have all this rain coming down outside and the taps stone dry. We've been carrying buckets in from the rainwater tank at the back of the house.

I'm sorry to go on like this but it does get pretty depressing, trying to keep the house at least somewhat liveable. I wish

4

we could send some of this rain down to you. According to the newspapers you haven't had much at all and the temperatures in Ranchi are still above a hundred. I know it must be terrible and I don't like to complain about the weather up here when I know it's so much worse for you.

The boys are doing fine at school. I spoke to Mrs Edwards about Tim's science grade and she says he's pulled himself up to a B— this quarter which is a big relief. Michael is going to be in the talent show next month. Do you think you could try to make it up for that? It's on the 25th. I know you've got so much work down there but even if you can make it up for a few days I know it would do you a lot of good.

Oops! Already eleven and the chowkidar is waiting to take the mail. I promise to write more regularly.

With all my love,
Rachel

Frank is the superintendent of a mental home run by the church in Ranchi. It was started back in the 1800's before people had any idea of modern analysis and therapy. Frank took over in 1960, the year after we arrived in India. When I first saw the place it was really pretty grim, like stepping back into the dark ages. The former director of the home was an English minister named Rev. Whitson, who had lived most of his life in India and really had no idea of mental health care. He was a caricature of the Victorian sahib and seemed to fit right in amidst the dark brick buildings and squalid drains. There was an old electroshock machine which looked like something out of the laboratory of a mad scientist. The cells in which the patients lived were like dungeons. Frank has changed a lot of that and built a new wing with pleasant wards and even a few private rooms. The really dingy cells have been turned into storage and the bars have been taken off all but a few of the windows. Frank has always been opposed to the idea of electroshock and the machine was really on its last legs anyway. It used to give a jolt to the attendants as well as the patients. There are so many new drugs these days which are just as effective. Frank also got the staff reorganized so that the home was more efficiently run, with better services. There's a visiting doctor and two full time nurses as well, who look after the patients. Frank is the only psychiatrist at the home but he has a couple of social workers who've done a course or two in counselling.

We took over Rev. Whitson's bungalow which was located in one corner of the compound, within the high boundary walls, which have broken glass along the top to keep anyone from climbing in or out. I didn't want to live there from the start, it was so depressing. Fortunately, our first year in India, the mission sent us up to the hills for language study which helped me get used to the idea of living inside a mental home. It's not that madness really bothers me. Frank has got me over all those fears but it's more the sense of timeless frustration. I think that Rev. Whitson had been affected by the job. He was very odd, a morbid little man who always seemed as though he was going to fall down on his knees and pray. When Frank took over there was a farewell function at which several of the inmates put marigold garlands around Rev. Whitson's neck and one of the staff made a flowery speech. We heard later that a few months after reaching England he committed suicide, which added to the gloominess of the place.

The first thing Frank did was change the name from "Christian Lunatic Asylum" to "Christian Home for the Mentally Disabled". He also went over all the files and released six epileptics who had no reason for being there and several others with only mild disorders. I worked with the maintenance staff to try and brighten up the compound. Unlike most Englishmen, Frank's predecessor had taken no interest in gardening.

The flower beds were full of weeds. Within the first year we planted hedges and quite a few lemon and grapefruit trees, revived the bougainvillea which grew along the walls and started a kitchen garden near the tube-well. Many of the patients were healthy enough to help in the gardens and I put them to work weeding and watering.

My other project was the kitchen, which was in a terrible state. The coal-burning stoves had blackened everything and there was grease all over the walls. For a whole week we did nothing but wash and scrub. I threw out all the pots and pans. I would have torn down the place completely if Frank hadn't been there to stop me. He kept saying that we couldn't change it all at once. I don't think Rev. Whitson had ever inspected the kitchen or else I underestimated his indifference. The stench of rotting vegetables and rancid oil clung to the kitchen even after it was painted.

Gradually the home became less like a prison and more hospitable, though it always had a feeling of imprisonment and despair. The hardest part of it for me were the patients. They had suffered so much and it was difficult to even begin to understand their problems. Frank used to say that he could diagnose a schizophrenic in America within five minutes, but here it was almost like talking to a person from another planet. There are rooms in the home which he has never let me visit. We used to argue about it in the beginning but after a while I saw that there was a real look of warning in Frank's eyes when he spoke about those patients, as though they were not just beyond curing but inhabited the darkest corners of madness.

Frank is an idealist. During his first year in medical school, he made up his mind that even though he was going to specialize in psychiatry, he wasn't going to become an ordinary analyst who charges by the hour. He wanted to do something to help people who really needed his care. Both of us were members of a church in Chicago which supported several

7

missionaries and I think that's how he got the idea of coming to India. We talked a lot about it before we got engaged and I told him that if he wanted to become a missionary I'd go with him wherever he went. It was something that mattered to him a great deal and he used to say how psychiatry had become a dirty business in America, like selling insurance or used cars, and so many people were in it just for the money. I know that's true. We visited one of Frank's old classmates on our last furlough. You've never seen such a house, with three cars in the garage, and a television in every room. It was a little disgusting to think that somebody could make all that money from other people's anxieties.

Frank applied to the mission board as soon as he began his internship. They weren't so sure about hiring a psychiatrist but asked if he could work as an M.D., since he had the qualifications. There were a lot of letters back and forth and it just happened that the mental home in Ranchi needed somebody around the time that Frank finished up his internship. Before I knew it, we were on our way.

I don't really regret that we came to India and Frank is very happy here. He feels as though he's doing something worthwhile instead of treating neurotic housewives and anorexic teenagers. It's not that they don't need help too but I think Frank has always been more interested in serious disorders, people who have really lost their sanity, patients who've gone beyond unhappiness and anxiety into another world.

Even though I trusted Frank's decision and I was proud of him for standing up for his principles, I always knew that the mental home in Ranchi was not a place to raise my children. There was just something so desolate about the place, so inhuman, so grotesque. I know it's terrible to think that way, to look at madness as an infectious disease, but I can't help it.

We go down to Ranchi during the winter holidays and spend three months with Frank. The boys don't seem to care.

8

They play with some of the patients and get them to make toys for them in the woodworking shop. Frank says there's nothing wrong with it. Maybe they will end up having a healthier attitude towards the mentally handicapped, but I'm still afraid. There are some things you can't get used to and I refuse to let my children spend the best years of their lives amongst a lot of suicidal, desperate people. It's just not fair on them.

The mission has a number of houses on the hillside which families can rent and use as summer cottages. Women start arriving around the beginning of May and usually remain up here until the end of September. That's the "hot season" on the plains. The men stay down and sweat it out, except for a week or two in June or July when they come up to be with their families. It's something of a missionary tradition, all of the memsahibs migrating up to the hillside like flocks of geese flying to Siberia.

We have always lived in Murchison, ever since Tim was old enough for kindergarten. It's a small cottage about half a mile above the school. The boys don't mind the walk and it has a nice view of the valley. Murchison gets its name from one of the old missionaries who came out to India sometime around 1875 and set up a Christian press for printing tracts and Bible literature. There's a picture of him in the dining room which was hanging there from before we moved into the house. Rev. Murchison looks very stern and full of conviction with bristly white hair and a flowing beard, one of the original missionary sahibs. I look at the picture and wonder sometimes if Frank will ever get like that, an ancient mariner, old and cragged and with a halo of white hair around his face.

Rev. Murchison built the cottage for his wife who died of typhoid soon after it was finished. He lived in it as a widower for many years and when he finally retired the mission took it over. They added a few rooms on either side to make it big enough to house a family. At some point they must have put in the plumbing and electricity. It's a funny old house and gets very damp during the monsoon. The inner rooms are dark, even though I've tried to brighten them up with curtains and pictures on the walls. At one time I thought I'd take the picture of Rev. Murchison down from his place of honour, but that would be a kind of sacrilege. He's like the presiding spirit of the house, very solemn and patriarchal.

Whenever we go back to the States on furlough, which is once every three years, I always get a shock at how clean and well-lighted the homes can be, not at all like Murchison. It makes me feel as though I've been living in a cave with all this dreary furniture and the leaks in the roof. Coming back to the hillside after we've been away on furlough, I get so depressed. I just want to have a home where the kitchen doesn't stink of charcoal smoke and the toilets flush and the cupboards aren't full of mildew and the walls don't peel and there aren't any spiders in the bookshelves.

I'm tired of living as a memsahib and I worry that I am getting to be like Lois Keck. She's such a fixture on the hillside. I wonder if, after the boys have graduated from school and gone back to America, I will keep on coming up to Murchison and live here by myself while Frank stays down in Ranchi all year long. Somehow, it frightens me, as though I am becoming like the picture of Rev. Murchison hanging up there year after year and nobody willing to take me down.

Some day I think the cicadas will drive me crazy. At times they get so loud I can't hear myself think, especially just around dusk. One starts and then another. Pretty soon there's a whole chorus of them. It's like a constant ringing in my ears which gets louder and louder until I want to hold my head and scream. They have a grating, metallic sound as if someone were scouring pots and pans. Outside my bedroom window there's an oak tree and the cicadas seem to like it there. I've tried to spot them lots of times but it's impossible to tell where the sound is coming from, the cicadas are so well camouflaged and hide inside the moss. Sometimes they are so loud that you have to shout to make yourself heard. The only thing that silences them is the rain on the tin roof because it's even louder. I just can't stand the racket which they make, all day and night. Michael brought a cicada home one time and showed it to me. It was kind of pretty, with its mottled green shell and transparent wings. He knew all about it from his science class, how they have smaller wings beneath the larger ones and how those rub against their shells and make a noise. Lyle Osborne, his science teacher, has got him interested in natural history. Michael is always coming home with things, porcupine quills or beetles, strange coloured lichens and bits of bark. I don't really mind since I know it's just healthy curiosity but I had to draw the line when he came home with a snake the other day.

'But Mom, it's a Graceful Dhaman,' he said, holding it up for me to see.

'I don't care what it is, you take it outside and let it go.'

'They aren't poisonous,' said Michael.

'How do you know for sure?' I said.

'Mr Osborne showed us how to tell. You see the scales on its stomach? When they're like that, straight across, it means it isn't poisonous.'

'Well, whatever it is, I just don't want it in the house.'

'But I want to take it to school tomorrow.'

'Michael, I don't want to hear any more arguments,' I said. 'Now take that snake back to where you found it and set it free.'

He looked disheartened but slowly turned around and went outside. I felt bad making him do it but I don't think I would have been able to go to sleep knowing that there was a snake inside the house.

I don't like the monsoon. It's beautiful of course when every-thing turns green, the trees get covered with shaggy moss, and the pushta walls are overgrown with ferns and orchids. For the first few weeks it seems like magic, the way the hillside changes after the dry months of May and June. All the dust gets washed away and things start popping out of the ground, mushrooms and fiddle-sticks, polypods and lichens. It's as though the forest comes back to life. There's always a frightening feeling about the rain hammering on the tin roof and the gutters spewing waterfalls into the yard. The paths turn into rivers and there's so much rain that the ground can't absorb it all. After the summer months, with the danger of forest fires and the dust haze in the air, the monsoon is a big relief. But after a while the excitement dies away and the leaks in the roof start appearing and I have to run around finding enough buckets and pans to put under the drips. It's as though the rain is just so hard, it penetrates everything. That's when I start to get depressed. The mist rolls in and the screens on the window are beaded with moisture. If you open a door, you can feel the dampness in the air, just blowing in.

Everything gets damp, the floors, the walls. There's mildew in the cupboards and shoes never seem to get completely dry. The house has a damp, unpleasant smell. Tick comes inside soaking wet and shakes himself on the carpet. He starts to stink and the whole house takes on the odour of wet dog. Even when I get into bed at night the sheets feel damp and the pillows have a musty smell. The moisture seems to get into everything. The doors and cupboards won't close; the woodwork swells up; barrel bolts and hinges get rusty; the salt shakers won't pour and the matches won't light; the bread gets mold on it and if you leave cookies on a plate for even a few minutes they turn soggy.

It's a bad time of the year for me because everything seems to go wrong. The dhobi never brings our laundry on time because he hasn't been able to get the clothes dry. Some days the mist gets so thick you have to turn on the lights to be able to see indoors, even during the middle of the day. Tim and Michael tramp mud into the living room, their umbrellas dripping puddles on the floor. They also have a way of losing umbrellas at school or coming back with someone else's.

And then there are all the crawling things as well, not just snakes, but scorpions and spiders. And the spiders aren't little things. They're huge and some of them have white egg sacks which look like ping pong balls. If you step on one by accident the sack bursts open and millions of tiny spiders come scurrying out. You have to be careful of the scorpions because they get into your clothes and shoes and I always remember to shake mine out before I put them on. There are leeches too. I hate them most of all because they drop off once they're engorged and then they lie there oozing blood all over the floor. Every time I go outside during the monsoon, I'm afraid of getting leeches. You can actually see them on the path, amongst the leaves, their heads waving up at you.

There is an oppressive feeling about the monsoon, as though nature is taking its revenge on us for having tried to settle here. More than any other time of the year I feel alone and helpless on the hillside. Everything becomes a jungle, even the flowerbeds and window boxes. The plants grow so high they can't support themselves and the rain beats them down. The dahlias get waterlogged and the gladiolas bend over as though submitting to the force of the monsoon. The weeds go out of control and I don't even try to tend the garden. It just goes wild. The only flowers which seem unaffected by the rain are the peacock orchids which grow everywhere, their pale lavender blossoms scattered amidst the tangle of green. There is an uncontrollable fertility in the mountains, as though the whole hillside, the red-roofed cottages, the winding trails and

13

parapet walls will soon be swallowed up by the jungle. Sometimes I imagine the trees growing closer and closer, the vines coming in over the windowsills and down the chimney, the doorframes sprouting leaves and the forest overwhelming the house like one of those ancient ruins. I can imagine myself having to hack away the shrubbery to get outside and being strangled by creepers.

CHAPTER 2

OKHRA FRITTERS   **Esther Rainey**

2 cups okhra (lady fingers)   1/8 tsp. salt
3 eggs   pepper to taste
2 oz. cheese   4 tsps. fat

Chop okhra into one inch pieces and boil in salted water. While okhra is cooking, beat eggs and add grated cheese to eggs. Drain okhra and mix with egg, cheese and seasoning. Heat fat in frying pan and drop spoonfuls of the mixture into the fat. Fry until crisp and golden brown on both sides. Serve hot.

Yesterday we had a meeting of the cookbook committee at Esther Rainey's house. She's the president of our Women's Club, one of the Methodist ladies. I don't like her very much. She has to poke her nose into everything I'm doing and interferes a lot. After all, I am the editor and this cookbook is my responsibility. Esther is always asking stupid questions and making suggestions which only add to the confusion. Last time we met, she wanted to know why we didn't organize the book into separate menus instead of different sections for poultry, breads and meat. We wasted half an hour discussing this and when we put it to a vote, she was the only person who wanted it that way. Even then, she wasn't resigned to our decision and kept saying how she found it easier to have a whole meal printed on one page instead of turning back and forth from one section to another.

Everybody has their own ideas about the book but most of the women on the committee are reasonable, not like Esther. I try to run the meetings fairly and give everyone a chance to speak, but it's difficult with Esther trying to dominate. She really isn't even supposed to be a member of our committee but being president, she's decided to make herself ex-officio. Already she's given me twenty recipes and says she has some more. None of them are very interesting and I wouldn't dare to try them on my boys. Esther's son, Richard, is in Michael's class. They've never got along and Michael says he's "such a slob". I sometimes wish that I could be as honest as Michael. He makes up his mind about people and isn't afraid to say what he feels. I'd love to call Esther some kind of name. It's terrible having to be so polite and nice to everybody all the time. That's what I hate most about the hillside, all the stupid pleasantries which we put up with, smiling till our jaws ache. We're all supposed to be good Christian ladies, charitable and sweet-natured. But sometimes, I just want to be a bitch and tell Esther Rainey that her recipe for Okhra Fritters sounds like instant leftovers.

The meeting took much longer than usual because we had to discuss the weights and measures. I thought we had already decided that we would convert everything to cups and spoons, but the British women insist on giving fluid ounces, while dear old Betsy Cullens has gone metric, bless her soul. What makes me really mad is that I'd made a point of telling everybody in the last meeting that we'd be using cups and spoons; but nobody listens, especially not when it means they have to do a little extra work. My math is so weak I can't even help the boys with their homework, leave aside make all of these conversions on my own.

It wasn't until half past twelve that I was able to get away. Esther lives in Vincent Lodge which is at the bottom of the hill, a long walk up to Murchison. I was almost running on the way home because I had to go to Renuka Sen's for lunch. She's a friend of mine who lives on the north side of the hill and I had promised her that I would be there by twelve.

When I got home it was almost one and I wanted to change into something more comfortable. Even though I knew that Renuka wouldn't mind if I was late, it made me angry and impatient. The cookbook meeting had upset me and I wanted nothing more to do with Esther and her stupid ideas. After pulling on my new block-printed cotton dress, I came outside to find the mutton wallah had arrived and wanted to be paid because he was going off to his village for a week. I told him there wasn't a single rupee in the house and he would have to wait until the chowkidar got back from the bank. He seemed disappointed but nodded solemnly, quite willing to wait all day. I hate it when I'm in a rush and there are people all around me with so much time on their hands.

Going around the corner of the house, I stepped on Tick who likes to lie in the flowerbeds. He yelped but I was too angry to even shout at him, furious with myself for being late.

Renuka isn't one of us. That's probably why I like her. She lives at Erinfell, which she has been renting from the Baptists for the past six years, a nice little cottage on the north side of the hill. She lives alone except for one servant, an old hill woman named Savitri. Renuka is something of a free spirit, older than me by a couple of years. She writes poetry and gave a reading at the Women's Club two years ago. I didn't understand too much of it but there was a nice feeling to the words. Some of the women felt she was a bit romantic and one or two thought the poems were obscene, but that's not really something you can judge if a person is writing from her heart. After the reading, I went up and told her how much I liked what she had written. There was something very natural and pleasant about Renuka and we got along at once. Most of the

17

other women treated her with caution. There aren't too many Indian ladies in the Women's Club, except for Mrs Emmanuel Das and Sheila Thomas. Sometimes I think Renuka is like an exotic bird of paradise in a cage full of sparrows. Maybe I'm exaggerating, but there is a quality about her which makes me realize how isolated and petty the hillside really is.

Renuka is a striking woman to look at, whether she is dressed up in a sari or wearing blue jeans and T-shirt as she does around the house. Renuka is quite tall, almost six feet. She has very long hair, without a streak of grey, which she usually keeps pinned at the back of her neck. Her face is plain, except for her eyes which she darkens with antimony. They have an expressive intensity, disturbing almost, like her poems. She wears less jewelry than most Indian women but always gold, usually a pair of earrings and a thin chain around her throat.

Renuka went to school in convents and did her college in Calcutta. She speaks English with such a clear and fluid accent, though she writes all of her poems in Bengali. Renuka says that it's a much more poetic language and though she has translated some of her writings into English, she claims it's never quite the same. Even though I don't understand the words, I love to hear her recite her poems in Bengali, the words have such a musical rhythm and her voice takes on a whole different personality. Renuka is so cultured compared to all of us, so well-read, so artistic. I always feel like a Minnesota farm girl when I am talking with her. Renuka seems to have so much within her, so much understanding, so many different experiences.

Even though I met her several times after the poetry reading it was only last year, when I came up with the boys at the beginning of March, that the two of us became close friends. There were very few women on the hillside at that time of year. March was cold and wet, with even a little snow. Renuka had spent the whole winter at Erinfell and she told me how it was her favourite time of year, with most of the houses locked up and the bazaar deserted. We met each other a few days after I arrived on the hillside and she seemed eager for company. Renuka came over to our house at least two or three evenings a week and if the boys had finished their homework we would play Scrabble around the big wood-burning bukhari which Bindru kept lit all day in the sitting room. Renuka is an expert at Scrabble and she usually won without much competition. The boys enjoyed her visits as much as I did and it would take a lot of persuasion to get them off to bed. After the boys had gone to bed I would make a pot of coffee and we would sit up for hours. Renuka would talk and I would listen and the time seemed to slip by like water flowing under a bridge. But no matter how late it was, Renuka would always walk home to Erinfell, even though I offered to make a bed for her on the sofa or let her sleep in my room. Even on nights when there was no moon, she never carried a torch, setting off in the dark by herself.

'I've got cat's eyes, Rachel,' she would say. 'I can see without a light.'

It was during those first few months last year, when the hillside was still uncrowded and the nights were cold and silent, that I really grew close to Renuka in a way that I never imagined possible. When I was in school and college I had a number of friends. Even now I still send Christmas cards to my old room-mate, Alice Jennings, who married a lawyer from Duluth. But as soon as Frank came into my life all other friendships seemed to end, as though marriage precluded any other relationship at all. It's a strange thing to think about. I've really never had any friends amongst the other women on the hillside, even though we pretended to be 'Sisters in Christ'. There is that kind of pious amity, which sets my teeth on edge.

19

These are false friendships, at least for me, and I never imagined that I would come to find someone like Renuka. During those late March evenings, with the sound of the octave owl in the oak tree outside the window and the bukhari growing cold because I had forgotten to stoke the fire, I found myself listening to Renuka as though we had been friends forever. I could sense a bond between us, as though our lives had come together not by chance, but as if we had found each other after years of searching. Nothing I have ever known with anyone, not even Frank, could match the intimacy of those evenings by the fire.

Renuka was always unpredictable and impulsive. She would exhaust me with her enthusiasm, talking constantly about some book she'd read or some memory which had been jogged in her mind. When I was with her there was an irresistible excitement to her words, her imagination. If I hadn't known her better, I might have called it childishness, the way she threw herself upon me without restraint. She had a way of overcoming my inhibitions.

I don't think there is anyone who could make me feel as happy and lighthearted as Renuka. Whenever I was with her things which worried me all day became unimportant. After visiting her, I would feel embarrassed because I'd laughed so hard. She had a way of making everything seem comical, especially the other women on the hillside. She could be very wicked sometimes and her imitations of Esther Rainey were absolutely devastating. I never knew anybody who had such a gift for mimickry.

There were times when I wondered why she had chosen to be my friend. Her life had been so full of strange and exotic experiences. I felt quite plain in comparison.

I fell in love with Renuka — there is no other way of saying it. I admired her in a way that surprised me sometimes. Even though I had lived in India for twelve years, I had never really met an Indian woman before, except in brief, uneasy encounters over tea and biscuits. Actually, I never thought of Renuka as Indian or anything else, except herself, as if she belonged to a country all her own.

'What does your name mean?' I once asked her.

'It has something to do with motherhood and purity,' she said. 'Renuka was the mother of Parasu Rama, the sixth incarnation of Vishnu. According to the legends she began to think impure thoughts which annoyed her husband, Jamad agni. I don't know what these impure thoughts could have been, the legend doesn't say. Anyway, she had five sons and the youngest was Parasu Rama. Her husband asked each of the sons to kill their mother. The first four refused but Parasu Rama obeyed and chopped off his mother's head with an axe. Like all mythology it has its gruesome moments. The father was so pleased, he granted Parasu Rama a boon and the devoted son asked that his mother be restored to life, with a pure mind and no recollection of her death.'

'What a frightening story,' I said.

'Now you know why I never got married,' said Renuka. 'I've always been afraid of having my head chopped off.'

'Is that really the reason?' I said, teasing her.

'Not exactly,' said Renuka. 'My parents tried very hard to get me married off and for a short time I was engaged to a well known lawyer in Calcutta.'

I kept quiet but Renuka could easily read my mind.

'You're too polite to ask me more,' she said. 'Rachel, please, I have nothing to hide from you. Just imagine, if I hadn't put my foot down, I would have become Mrs Honourable Justice Ganguly. He became a judge in the Calcutta High Court.'

'What made you change your mind?'

'I don't know,' said Renuka. 'Intuition. I suddenly realized that he was a fucking bastard.'

Stopping herself, she covered her mouth.

'Oh, damn, I'm sorry, Rachel,' she said, 'I keep forgetting that you're a missionary.'

'Don't be silly,' I said, trying not to look embarrassed. 'Your language doesn't bother me.'

'I would call him worse, if I had the vocabulary,' said Renuka. 'I never regretted breaking off the engagement, even though my father was outraged. He couldn't understand why I didn't like the man.'

'What was wrong with him?' I said.

'He was just a pompous ass. I was eighteen and he was thirty-five and thought he was the most handsome creature in Bengal, with long sideburns and a little moustache. He always wore a black suit and waistcoat and one of those little white bibs. From the first time I met him, I noticed that there was something odd about his hair but it wasn't until one day, several weeks after we were engaged, that I realized he was completely bald on top. He must have spent hours each morning combing his hair to cover it up. We were sitting on the verandah of my parents' house and a breeze came along and blew it all aside. He looked so silly with these long strands of hair hanging over one ear and a clean dome on top. I couldn't help but laugh and he was terribly offended. Of course, that wasn't the only reason I disliked him. There was something slimy about him. He would tell me that he wanted me to be a "modern wife" — I don't know what he meant by that — and he would hold my hand and say he loved me. Just imagine, we'd only known each other for a couple of weeks and he was pretending it was some great romance.'

'I bet a lot of men have been in love with you,' I said.

'Maybe. But I was never interested. I find most men are disappointing. They take themselves so seriously.'

Renuka had opened the subject herself and even urged me to pry into her past, but she was quick to close herself away again and that was all she told me of her engagement, a brief, unhappy brush with marriage.

When Tim and Michael first met Renuka, they didn't know what to think of her. She overpowered them with her curiosity, asking questions about their school, what books they read, what sort of things they learned in class. She told them that they should read Mark Twain. Renuka was insistent and kept saying that it was important for them, because they needed to understand their own culture. The next day she sent a coolie to the house with two copies of his books, *Huckleberry Finn* for Michael and *A Connecticut Yankee in King Arthur's Court* for Tim, each inscribed with her careful handwriting:

To Michael,

   The Mississippi is as great a river as the Ganga.

                    With all my love, Renuka.

To Tim,

   The ultimate American fantasy, exiled in time!

                    With all my love, Renuka.

I didn't think the boys would appreciate or understand what she had written to them but I was amazed when I found that both of them were actually reading the books. Neither of them is much of a reader but Renuka seemed to inspire them, the same way she inspired me, with her irrepressible enthusiasm.

When I finally got to Renuka's house, it was raining heavily and my shoes were soaked. She waved away my apologies with a careless hand and when I kissed her cheek, I could smell alcohol on her breath. I knew that Renuka drank and once or twice she had offered me something, though I always refused. Actually, I'm not a puritan about these things. My father used to enjoy his beer and we would have wine at

23

the table on special occasions, but here on the hillside it is
taboo. I think that even if I suggested putting a little wine or
sherry in one of the cookbook recipes, a lot of women would
get upset.

'What about a hot rum with lemon?' said Renuka. 'I'm
having one.'

She pointed to her glass, which was almost empty.

I shook my head.

'Rachel, don't be such a prude,' she said. 'Nobody's watching. Your husband is far away.'

'I really don't like the taste,' I said. 'That's all.'

'But it's good for you on a day like this,' said Renuka. 'Keeps
you from catching a cold.'

She went inside the kitchen, taking her own glass with
her. I sat down and caught my breath after the hurried walk.
It was always nice to come to Renuka's. She never invited
anyone else but me and it was such a relief after all those
awful women's luncheons, with everybody nattering at once
and the feeling that each of us was trying frantically to talk
our way out of a corner — the usual gossip about those women
who hadn't come up to the hills this year, servant problems,
endless talk of children and school. Instead of that, Renuka
always had something so much more interesting to discuss.
She would reminisce about Calcutta or talk about her poetry.
She had done a great many things and seemed to have lived a
very glamorous life before she came to the hillside.

Her living room was full of different things which she'd col-
lected, a wonderful jumble of objects and pictures. There were
some modern paintings on the walls which I didn't particularly
like but also a set of miniatures that she told me had belonged
to her father. They were very old and some of them had water
stains or were torn at the edges, but the colours remained
vivid and the pictures were so intricate, tiny horsemen riding
out to battle, palaces of red sandstone, and one picture of an

elephant rearing up to stamp on a tiger while the hunters on its back held on for dear life. Their expressions were so finely drawn. Renuka also had a bronze statue of a dancing figure in one corner, and a stone carving which had always surprised me, of a couple making love, their legs and arms entangled in an impossible embrace. She called them her 'petrified lovers'. I knew that the miniatures and the statues had to be antiques but in the midst of these really valuable works of art, Renuka also had a variety of things which she'd picked up from her walks around the hillside, such as a curiously shaped stick which she had polished and hung from a nail on the wall. It looked like a magician's wand. There was an assortment of pinecones and pieces of bark, snail shells, a dried bouquet of flowers in a wine bottle, an old porcelain chamber pot in which she kept her magazines. Renuka's house was so much a part of her character, full of interesting things but always untidy and disorganized.

Renuka had a number of photographs as well, one of her mother and father and one of herself as a younger woman, looking very elegant, in a brocade sari and lounging on a low divan. I always enjoyed seeing that photograph because she looked so confident and beautiful, almost like a maharani. The room was also full of books, one whole wall covered with shelves, filled to overflowing. The lights in the room were dim, except for a reading lamp which stood beside one chair where she always sat. None of the furniture matched but there was a feeling that she had chosen everything quite carefully. It was the sort of room which only a single person can have, so full of individuality and secrets.

Renuka claimed that Erinfell was haunted. I wasn't really sure whether she was serious or just making it up. There was certainly a mysterious atmosphere about the cottage, tucked away on the north side of the hill, with its low eaves and dark wood floors. According to Renuka the house had once belonged to a British army officer who used to come up to the hills for hunting expeditions. He had been a great shikari and there were even a few antlers and bear skulls left over from his trophy collection. Renuka said that he had died when one of his guns went off by accident while he was cleaning it. I don't know where she got the story but Renuka said that the Englishman still haunted the place and sometimes at night she would hear a gunshot far down in the valley. Her servant Savitri was also convinced that there was a ghost in the house. Renuka said that two years ago Savitri almost quit because she had seen a figure pacing back and forth on the verandah. Renuka had finally agreed to get one of the priests from the bazaar to perform a special puja. The priest had told her that because the ghost was an Englishman she would have to give him an offering of two bottles of whisky. Renuka had refused at first, knowing that the priest planned to drink it himself, but when Savitri became hysterical and said that she wouldn't work in the house for another day unless the priest did the puja, Renuka relented. There was a goat which had to be purchased for the sacrifice and all of the servants from the hillside came to watch the puja which was held at Erinfell. One of the chowkidars cut off the goat's head with a big chopper. Renuka said that she hadn't been able to watch them actually behead the goat and stayed indoors while that was happening. The bottles of whisky were offered to the spirituous Englishman — Renuka swore the priest drank most of it and only poured a little bit on the front steps of the verandah as a kind of libation. Renuka laughed when she told me about the whole thing but she said that they'd had no more trouble from the ghost since that time. The sacrifice had brought trouble, though, from another quarter. When the Baptists heard what was going on, they were irate and threatened to throw Renuka off the property if she held another puja at Erinfell. Renuka said that there had been a big fuss about it and several of the Baptist ladies had called on her to express their disapproval.

The hot rum and lemon which Renuka brought for me didn't taste half as bad as I expected, though I drank it cautiously, afraid that it would go straight to my head. I noticed that Renuka was in a reckless mood. She was wearing a loose caftan with Kashmiri embroidery around the collar and sleeves. Her hair was open and she kept brushing it back from her face, gesturing excitedly with her hands as she spoke.

Savitri served us lunch in the living room and Renuka tried to persuade me to have another rum. As we were eating she began to tell me about the recent, unexpected visit of a distant cousin, who had arrived two days ago. Renuka and he had played together as children. The cousin was now a married man, working for a textile company in Delhi. Renuka had hardly kept in touch with him but suddenly there he was at her doorstep, without any warning. He had heard from someone in the family that Renuka was living by herself and assumed that she was lonely. He took the weekend off and drove all the way from Delhi with the obvious intention of seducing her. Renuka found it very funny and told the story with a lot of laughter. Her cousin first tried to get her drunk but ended up quite tipsy himself. He told her how unhappy he was with his wife and kept putting his arm around her shoulder. Renuka stayed out of his reach as best she could and after dinner she said a quick goodnight. Her cousin seemed disappointed but said nothing. A little while later, just as she was falling asleep, he walked into her bedroom, completely naked. Renuka is very clever at imitations and she stood up and showed me exactly how her cousin had approached the bed, swaying drunkenly, with a lost expression in his eyes. When she told him to put his clothes back on and go to bed, he began to plead with her and kept saying how lonely she must be. It was only when she threatened to tell his wife and the whole family, that he finally left her alone. The next day he took off without even saying goodbye.

'Rachel, you don't know how funny it was,' she said.

'Weren't you frightened?' I asked.

'Of him? He was so pathetic. I knew he wouldn't try a thing,' said Renuka.

'I would have been terrified,' I said.

'It's strange how men are so naïve. They see that a woman is living alone and they imagine she must be desperate for sex. I mean there's no chance that they would think a woman might just want to remain a contented celibate.'

She said it in a flippant sort of way but I realized afterwards how the incident had bothered her more than she would admit. Renuka had a way of wanting to appear invulnerable.

CHAPTER 3

VINDALOO

Iris DeSouza

2 kilos pork
1 cup vinegar
3 teaspoons salt
5 cloves garlic
2 teaspoons ground ginger
1/2 cup mustard oil
2 medium sized onions
   (chopped)
2 sprigs curry patta

1 teaspoon whole coriander
1 teaspoon whole cumin
6 whole red chillies
2 tablespoons curry powder
(garam masala)
3 whole cardamons (green)
5 whole cloves

Cut and trim the pork into one inch cubes. Fry the onions in the mustard oil until they turn a reddish brown. Add whole spices, garlic and ginger, salt and curry powder. Fry for three to five minutes. Add pork, stirring slowly until the meat is well covered in the spices and begins to brown. Add vinegar and curry patta. Cover and cook over a slow fire. Add more vinegar or lemon juice if necessary but do not add water. Use a pressure cooker for quicker cooking. Pork Vindaloo can be served hot with rice and vegetables or cold as a meat pickle.

Mrs DeSouza runs a boarding house called Kisli Lodge. It's an old building that was once the summer home of the Nawab of Kisli. Mrs DeSouza's father used to be the bandmaster for the Nawab and when he retired the Lodge was given to him as a gift. Mrs DeSouza is now in her seventies but still very sharp and full of humour, a wonderful woman. She manages the boarding house by herself along with three servants whom she rules over with a shrill, insufferable voice. The building itself has a kind of ramshackle grandeur about it, though it isn't all that large. Mrs DeSouza has been running the boarding house for as long as I can remember. Frank and I stayed there during our first year on the hillside.

Mrs DeSouza is Anglo-Indian and she was married to an army officer who died in the second world war. Her husband was a Goan Catholic but she is Church of England and very proud of it. Her father's name was Henderson. She has no children of her own but several of her nieces and nephews have lived with her and attended the school. Every winter she closes up the boarding house and goes down to Bombay to stay with her sister.

Kisli Lodge is located just above the main bazaar with an enormous deodar tree in the front yard. There are about twelve rooms altogether and a large dining hall in which there is a portrait of Mrs DeSouza's father dressed up in his band uniform with a conductor's baton held up as if to signal the first beat of a military march. He looks very grand, with a thick moustache and pale green eyes. Mrs DeSouza — nobody calls her Iris — used to play the organ at church until a few years ago when her arthritis got too bad. She has a grand piano in the sitting room of Kisli Lodge and I remember she used to give lessons to some of the children from school and once in a while she would even give a recital.

There is something very quaint about the boarding house. It needs a good coat of paint and there is still no running hot water in the bathrooms. Mrs DeSouza has special rates for missionaries, about half the price she charges her other guests. She is a very religious woman and doesn't allow smoking or drinking on the premises. At meal times she sits at the head of one of the tables, and always asks one of the guests to say a blessing before the servants bring in the food. She used to do a lot of the cooking herself and nobody ever complained about the meals at Kisli Lodge. Nowadays Mrs DeSouza still spends a lot of time in the kitchen but her cook does most of the work.

I always enjoy hearing Mrs DeSouza tell stories about when she was young and the town was a popular hill station for the Maharajahs. There was a bandstand near the clocktower and every summer Mrs DeSouza's father and his band would perform, playing foxtrots and serenades while people rode past in their rickshaws or promenaded along the mall. Besides the Maharajahs a number of Britishers used to come up for the summer and there were masked balls and amateur theatricals. Mrs DeSouza used to be one of the beauty queens of the town and she showed me pictures once of herself in a long gown with feather trim, escorted by a soldier in dress uniform. When I asked her if that was her husband, she shook her head, but didn't tell me any more.

All new missionaries come up to the hillside for their first year to study Hindi at the language school. Frank and I arrived in 1960, straight off the ship in Bombay. Everything was very strange for me, the sights we saw from the train window on the journey up country, like a kaleidoscope of images that I had never dreamed of; buffaloes wallowing in the mud; sadhus on the railway platforms with their matted hair and beards, carrying tridents; camels and oxcarts; the dry, uneven landscape, with scattered villages, forts and temples; crowds of pilgrims dressed in bright coloured clothes with vermillion smeared on their foreheads; children with their heads shaved; peacocks in the mustard fields. I remember how excited and frightened I was on that first journey. After one night at a hotel in Bombay we boarded the train, with what seemed like a hundred coolies loading our boxes into the brake van and the sweet old

31

gentleman from the travel agency who handled everything and reassured us as we got into our compartment. I never thought we would make it but soon enough we were rattling along the rails and the bearers in white turbans brought our meals and endless pots of tea. I sat and stared out of the window the whole way, watching the sights slip past.

Early on the second morning we came in view of the mountains. I looked outside and there they were — the Himalayas — dark blue in the dawn light, like shadows against the sky. Along the side of the tracks I could see thickets of bamboo and dry river beds of white boulders. Frank was sleeping on the upper berth and I woke him up to see the mountains. They seemed so close and yet it took us hours to get there, the steam engine puffing in the distance, the soot blowing through the window and the bearer bringing bed tea at one of the little stations where we stopped. It seemed to take forever until we finally reached the end of the line. The faces on the platform were a blur as we came into the station and I could hear the brakes on the train squealing as we pulled to a stop. Mr and Mrs Estes, who were in our mission, were there to meet the train. We had never seen them before but they were the only white faces on the platform and they waved to us as the carriage came to a stop. Mr Estes came inside and shook hands with Frank. He said that he had brought his jeep and trailer to take us up the hill and suggested that we have breakfast in the waiting room while he got the coolies to take our luggage out of the brake van and load it into the jeep.

Mrs Estes took both my hands in hers and welcomed me with a kiss, as though we were long lost relatives. She didn't let go of me until we sat down in the waiting room. I was feeling a little squeamish and had no appetite at all but Mrs Estes seemed anxious that I should have some breakfast. She ordered boiled eggs and toast for all of us. Frank had gone off with Mr Estes

32

to check on the luggage though I wished he would just stay beside me.

The Estes were from Pennsylvania and they had been in India for eighteen years. They were nice enough, maybe a little over-protective. Mrs Estes was one of those flighty, talkative women who told me everything about herself within the first fifteen minutes. Mr Estes was a much quieter, solemn man who leaned close to Frank every time he had anything to say as though it wasn't meant for me to hear. They had brought a thermos flask full of boiled water for us to drink and warned us about getting diarrhoea. On the train ride we had eaten everything the bearer brought us, and when I told Mrs Estes she was horrified.

After breakfast, which I hardly touched, we went out to the jeep. It was old and decrepit, a muddy green colour. Loaded up with all our luggage, it looked as though we were setting off on a safari. Frank and I got in the back and Mr and Mrs Estes rode in front. The jeep wouldn't start at first and Mr Estes had to get the coolies to give us a push. When the engine finally caught it made a terrible, roaring noise. There was a lot of smoke from the exhaust. Mrs Estes had tied a scarf around her head and she looked a little like a dowdy version of Ossa Johnson in Africa.

It's an hour's ride up the hill and the motor road twists and turns. Even though the jeep couldn't go very fast with the heavy load, I was terrified by the way Mr Estes swung around the corners, and one time when he overtook a truck I thought for sure that something was going to come around the corner and hit us before we got past. I was glad that Frank was beside me so that I could hold onto him. When we stopped halfway up the hill, to put some water in the radiator which was boiling over, I was glad to get out and stretch my legs. Mrs Estes offered us some coffee from another thermos — they seemed to have a whole collection of flasks. I was feeling light-headed from the

33

drive and when we got back into the jeep I put my head on Frank's shoulder and closed my eyes. It seemed as though the road was never going to end, around and around the corners. Each time I thought we were reaching the top, we'd see another ridge, higher up.

When we finally got to the bus stand in the bazaar, which was as far as the jeep could go, Mr Estes said that it was about two miles' walk to Kisli Lodge where we'd be staying. He suggested that I take a dandie, since I hadn't got my 'hill legs' yet. Pretty soon I saw four coolies arrive with a kind of sedan chair and I realized that I was going to have to ride in that. I was going to refuse but I was feeling really sick to my stomach now and two miles seemed a long way to walk. Frank helped me get into the dandie and before I knew it the coolies had picked me up and were carrying me away on their shoulders. They were all shouting and laughing amongst themselves. I yelled for Frank and he made the coolies stop. I felt terrible and Frank looked awfully embarrassed. There were so many people watching. It was the worst sort of arrival anyone could have. Mr Estes told Frank to go ahead with me and he would take care of the luggage. We set off, Frank on one side and Mrs Estes on the other. I remember flashes of the bazaar as we went through, the clock tower and one or two of the shops but I was feeling so sick by then, I didn't notice very much.

It must have been something which I ate on the train, because I was throwing up all night and stayed in bed for almost a week. I felt sorry for Frank, because he had to do all of the moving-in, on top of looking after me. Mrs DeSouza made me vegetable soup each day because that was about all I could eat. She still remembers how pathetic I was when I first arrived. 'Mrs Manton,' she says, 'I looked at you and I said to myself, this poor dear, she looks as though she wants to die. You were as pale as a ghost and I felt like telling your husband to take you home.'

As soon as I was feeling well enough to go out, Frank took me for a walk around the hillside. From Kisli Lodge it wasn't very far to the top of the hill and we made our way up the path quite slowly, stopping whenever I felt my legs go weak. It was early May, the weather clear and we could see out across the plains for quite a way. I was feeling more cheerful now and not so miserably homesick. A number of visitors had come to see me at Mrs DeSouza's and everyone had been very encouraging.

While we were resting at the side of the path, three or four children came by on their way to school. They greeted us politely and I couldn't help feeling as though we were back in America, the children's clothes, their accents, the way they swung their bookbags around and whistled at each other. It was like something out of Tom Sawyer except that we were seven thousand feet up in the Himalayas. A little further along the path we met a woman taking her cocker spaniel for a walk. She was also an American and when we introduced ourselves she said she'd heard that we were coming and asked if I was feeling better. It was like being in a small town where everybody knew all there was to know about each other.

When we finally got to the top of the hill, I was completely out of breath. Frank had told me about the view of the snow mountains but I wasn't at all prepared for what I saw. We came up onto the crest of the ridge. There were a few deodar trees on either side and in between were the snow peaks, like a picture cut out of a magazine, so huge and unbelievable. Even after twelve years, I still get that feeling of awe whenever I see the snows. On that first day, with my lungs aching and my legs about ready to collapse, I couldn't help but be emotional. It was like a vision, so white and dazzling in the morning sun. I put my arm around Frank and started to cry. He was a little surprised and pulled me close. I don't usually get like that but it was as though something broke inside of me. I'd reached the

35

top of the hill and there they were, enormous and eternal, as though we were in the presence of God.

Our room at Mrs DeSouza's was small but comfortable and we had a glassed-in verandah overlooking the bazaar. Like all hillside houses there were no double beds, two little cots with a dressing table in between. The first thing we did was shift the beds around so that they were side by side. We had been married for only eight months and that first year on the hillside was like an extended honeymoon. Neither of us had very much to do except attend our language classes. Frank helped out at the hospital from time to time but mostly we were free to study our vocabulary and grammar. Frank picked it up quite easily but I had a lot more trouble, especially with all the grammatical rules, the genders and so many different sounds, I got tongue-tied just trying to pronounce the words. We had tutorials together with two or three different language teachers. They were very patient with me, even though I didn't seem to be making any progress.

There were other language students staying at Kisli Lodge and we became friends with some of them. Connie and Ted Simpson arrived from Canada a few weeks after us. They were about our age and we got along quite well together and went for several hikes back into the mountains. Oddly enough, we really didn't need to use much Hindi on the hillside because there were so many Americans and the servants at Mrs DeSouza's spoke good English. I was able to communicate with the shopkeepers in the bazaar by sign language and the few words I began to pick up. During the first months, after I recovered from my illness, Frank and I had to go out to dinner almost every night. It was like doing the social rounds and we got a little tired of it after a while. The worst was having dinner with the Francis Mitchums, the senior missionaries on the hillside. They had two bearers in white pugarees and brass badges with 'F.M.' done in spiral lettering on their coat pockets. The

36

service was real china and we had a soup course and a fish course, roast chicken, and boiled potatoes. For dessert there was mango fool. I don't know why I should remember the menu after all these years, but it sticks in my mind, maybe because I couldn't get over the affected elegance of that evening. It was so odd to see American missionaries behaving like characters out of Rudyard Kipling, especially since it was 1960. I have resigned myself to a lot of things about being in India, but I could never live with all those manners and that little silver bell which Mrs Mitchum rang to call the bearers, when we had finished each course. My family are plain-spoken mid-western folks, farmers most of them, and I was never meant to be a memsahib.

Spread out along the top of the ridge, the town has only one main street running from the old bazaar to Shepherd's Bluff, about four miles in length. The buildings in the centre of town are built one on top of the other, a jumble of corrugated tin roofs and chequered windows. At night it looks like a winding procession of festive lights. Sometimes I think the town doesn't belong where it is, as if some flood had risen to the height of the ridge and then receded, leaving a trail of debris in its wake. The buildings are crooked and misshapen, perched helter-skelter on the few level patches of land. An unlikely place for anyone to have built a town, the mountains seemed to defy all human efforts at habitation. Looking down from Murchison, I often try to picture the place as it must have looked before there were any houses, a precipitous ridge with cliffs and cragged peaks, covered on the southern slopes by long grass and on the northern slopes by forests of oak and rhododendron.

On a monsoon day when the mist sweeps in and erases the town, I have often heard the barking deer on Jawala Tibba and listened for the shrill call of the whistling thrush. The tops of the ridges stand out like islands in the clouds and there is a feeling of wildness and isolation.

According to Mrs DeSouza the town used to be known as the most licentious hill-station in the Himalayas. Despite the present atmosphere of decay, there remains a suggestion of the opulence and gaiety which the British and the Maharajahs brought to it. The Ghazipur summer palace is still standing, a fairy-tale castle, complete with turrets, though most of the windows are shuttered tight and the park is overgrown with nettles. The Carlton Hotel and Stockton's, which were the most popular dancing establishments in their time, are now in shabby condition. The Maharajah of Baroda's estate is completely in ruins and the Nawab of Rampur's summer palace has been converted into a mushroom farm.

Beauty contests are still held at the Carlton and Stockton's Hotel has a floor show during the tourist season, but these are tawdry affairs. It's almost as though the excitement has left the town. There is an atmosphere of wasted charm and withered beauty. Of course, the postcards and tourist literature still proclaim it, 'Queen of Hills', but like the deposed royalty of India, the town has become an erstwhile Maharani.

By the time Frank and I arrived most of the Maharajahs had departed and the gates of their pleasure palaces had rusted shut. The town continued to emit an odour of forbidden fruit, overripe and close to rotting.

One evening, just for fun, Connie and Ted Simpson and Frank and I went to see a cabaret at Stockton's. If the senior missionaries had known what we were doing they would have been appalled. The dancer had some name like Salome and she was hideously fat, with folds of flesh around her belly and thighs which rippled when she moved. After doing an awkward strip-tease, she came and sat on Frank's lap. I've never seen him blush so red and we teased him about it afterwards. The only other people in the audience were a few inebriated businessmen. The dancer's costume consisted of several yards of silk chiffon, a head dress of peacock feathers and a glittering bikini. As she gyrated about, some of the sequins came loose and fell to the floor. The cabaret dancer made me think of a grotesque bird-of-paradise in moult. A crooner followed her performance with a medley of Cliff Richard favourites.

Nowadays a different kind of tourist visits the town. Instead of the royal families and courtiers, the summer visitors are mostly lower-level clerks and government servants who can't afford to splurge. For them, the town has had to adjust its style from fancy dress balls and beer gardens to cheaper entertainments and crowded little hotels. Many of the tourists are honeymoon couples, the brides still wearing their embroidered saris and the grooms with their moustaches standing on end. Photographers do a thriving business at all the scenic spots, Lookout Point, the Municipal Gardens, and Fern Falls. The honeymoon couples pose self-consciously for the camera, holding hands, or with their arms clasped around each other.

The 'hillside' is a much more sober place and stands to the east of the town, a steep, forested ridge which is roughly shaped like a loaf of bread. At the top of the ridge there are three rounded summits. Circling each summit, like three links in a chain, is a level bridle trail. This is called the 'chukker' and it is a quiet, scenic place to walk. You can see the snow mountains to the north and to the south, the plains stretch outwards in a mosaic of fields, bordered by the ragged line of Siwalik hills which are a much older range than the Himalayas, reduced to crumbling insignificance by century upon century of erosion.

Most of the hillside homes are built on the southern slope, facing the plains. A narrow trail runs laterally across the face of the ridge. This is called 'the Goat Path' because it is so narrow. At some places it is no wider than a foot and crosses a stretch of cliffs which are called 'the Crags'. The Goat Path connects many of the cottages with the town and passes the hospital and the Community Centre. At right angles is a steep road which twists back and forth, climbing the hill from the school to the chukker. There are many other trails criss-crossing the hillside from one house to the next and every path has at least three shortcuts, for those who don't mind scrambling up or down the khud.

The school is located roughly in the centre of the hillside, with dormitories and other buildings scattered below. The school dominates the hillside, a solid, imposing complex of red roofs and yellow walls. It looks something like a monastery, set amidst chestnut trees and deodars.

The hillside was originally a British cantonment where convalescent soldiers were sent to recover from their wounds and illnesses. The military hospital was closed down around the end of the last century and a lot of the properties were sold to American mission societies. The early missionaries adopted the British habit of sending their women and children to the hills during the summer months and after the school was built the hillside also became a centre for language study, where fresh young evangelists from Hiram, Ohio, and Poughkeepsie learned to preach the word of the Lord in Hindustani.

There are three churches at the top of the hill, including an old Catholic church which is now abandoned and desanctified. It looks like a bombed-out Grecian temple. A little lower down, on the south side of the hill, is St John's, the old cantonment church which still has notches in the pews where the British Tommies rested their Enfield rifles when they kneeled down to pray. Between the first and the second chukker is Hoburn Church which is where most of the families on the hillside worship. It is named for one of the early missionaries who helped translate the Bible into Hindustani and wrote one of the first Hindi grammars. According to the story Dr Hoburn was going for a walk and reading his Bible as he went along. Not looking where he was going he walked right off the edge of chukker and fell to his death.

Around the north side of the first chukker is the graveyard, shaded over with deodars and cypress. Some of the graves date back to the 1830's and most of them contain the bones of British officers and their families. There is an enormous cypress which stands near the entrance and was planted in 1876 by the Prince of Wales. The graveyard is a kind of historical sanctuary, the dates of birth and death etched in stone like a sacred chronology. Most of the stones are covered with moss, overgrown with ferns and wild orchids. The inscriptions are in memory of riding masters, colour sergeants and captains, young wives and infant children. The gates are usually locked to keep stray cattle from toppling the gravestones.

We inherited from the British not only their bungalows and institutions, the prerogatives of white sahibs, morning tea and tiffin carriers, but the whole concept of a hill-station. The hillside is a refuge for women who come here for the summer months, escaping the heat of the plains. According to tradition, the men remain at their posts, sweating over their duties in 110 degrees of heat. The early missionaries probably saw it as one more test of their endurance before God, another cross to bear. While the women pined away in the hills, the men-folk continued the work of the Lord with diligence and devotion. The whole arrangement suited their puritan nature; the white-man's burden, the sacrifice of bodily comforts and companionship. Certainly there must have been the backsliders, the mission doctor who let his hands stray over the nursing sister, the tail-gate evangelist who spilled his seed in the wayside dust. It's a hard life out in the boondocks, imagining your wife and kids up in the hills, cool and beautiful. You feel betrayed and lonely, devoured by mosquitoes and bed bugs, alone and unappreciated but above all, blessed in the

41

sight of God. The Himalayas must seem like heaven, rising out of the clouds, the pine-clad slopes, the cottages and your wife standing there at the screen door in her apron, cheeks flushed with anticipation, the birdsong and day lilies, the children coming home from school, while you lie there on the charpai stripped to your underpants, a wet towel on your forehead, fighting back the loneliness, fighting back the constant doubts, fighting back the urge to catch a train and come straight up to the hills. The only escape from those melancholy hours of desperation is to work, fighting the indolence with good, old-fashioned, roll-up-your-sleeves hard work, until you have earned your perspiration, until the malaise breaks like a fever and you can finally sleep again and dream in peace about your family up there in the sky amidst the peacock orchids and the wild ginger.

We are like a lost tribe which has settled on this distant hillside, wanderers who have finally come to rest amongst the oaks and rhododendrons, finding a suitable environment in which to put down our roots. I think there is an unspoken feeling amongst us that we are exiles founding a new utopia in the wilderness, sons and daughters of the pioneers. The hillside is a cross between a British hill-station and a prairie town in the heartland of America. Many of the characters are the same, as are the rituals, the pleasantries of a small town and the underlying ugliness, the falsehoods, the gossip and the sense of isolation. It's all there. Amongst us there are visionaries and prophets, there are do-gooders and holy joes, and maybe even a few Christians. There are frauds and people with perverted vanities, there were recluses and wierdoes. There are Mennonites and Baptists, the Assemblies of God and Pentecostals, Methodists and Anglicans, Presbyterians and unknown little denominations with their own peculiar theologies. They are all here together on this hillside, an unusual assortment of castaways. We live by a separate, unwritten code. Each of us understands the importance of gamexene for killing silverfish, and the advantages of potted geraniums because they survive neglect. We accept the inevitability of the monsoon and the delicate forms of speech, such as saying 'shoot' instead of shit and 'darn' for damn. Each of us knows which snow peak is Vishwa Parbat and how it takes about a week after you arrive before you get your 'hill legs', and that the only way to get rid of a leech is to cover it with salt until it oozes blood all over the floor.

Every summer the mothers come up and take their children out of boarding. The hillside comes alive with families and servants, the sound of women shouting down the khud, calling their children home to dinner, or scolding the cook for breaking a new blender, or yelling at the dudhwallah for mixing water with his milk and haggling with the Kashmiri hawkers who come door to door, selling napkins and tea cosies. Everywhere you look there are memsahibs, walking back and forth from school, riding dandies, pouring tea. And once or twice a year the fathers come up for just a week or two, taking a holiday from their mission compounds on the plains, exhausted and disgruntled.

It seems as if everything was established long ago, a particular way of life which only exists on the hillside. Anyone who lives here is expected to abide by an unwritten code of conduct. Like any isolated community, the hillside is full of prejudices and each year the controversies break out with all kinds of accusations and arguments. The different denominations fight over school dances and fundamentalist theology, scriptural interpretations and the hillside water supply, the maintenance of paths and whether evolution science should be taught at the school. On the surface of course there is always a veneer of Christian fellowship and fraternity, but underneath there is conflict and acrimony, bigotry and intolerance.

CHAPTER 4

TRIFLE   **Connie Simpson**

One pound cake
2 cups strawberry jelly (Jello)
1 cup whipped cream
1 tin fruit cocktail
hundreds and thousands for decoration

Cut the pound cake into three inch pieces and put in a glass bowl with layers of jelly, fruit cocktail and whipped cream. Ingredients should mix together nicely. Cover with a layer of whipped cream and decorate with hundreds and thousands. Should be served soon after preparation.

Tick had been missing for two days and I was getting a little worried. There was supposed to be a leopard on the hillside which had carried off a couple of dogs. Tick doesn't stray very often and I had a feeling that there was probably a female in heat somewhere around and he was after her. The last time it happened Bindru found him all the way down in the bazaar, his neck chewed up from having had a fight and looking very bedraggled. I don't know what gets into dogs. Most of the time Tick just lies around and doesn't move a muscle unless it's time for food. But then all of a sudden, as soon as there's a scent of some female in heat, he's off and running. The only other thing that gets him excited are the monkeys which come around the hillside. He loves to chase them and they just sit in the trees and look down at him while Tick will bark and bark. I've never known a less intelligent dog.

After he didn't show up the second morning Michael was almost in tears. He was sure that the leopard had eaten Tick. I promised that I would go out and look for him. Even though I knew there wasn't much point, I set off a little after breakfast and spent about an hour wandering around the top of the hill, whistling and calling his name. Then I remembered Connie Simpson had a female labrador and that was the next place I tried. Sure enough, there were about six dogs in the yard, Tick amongst them. He came up and greeted me, looking awfully guilty. The other dogs were growling at each other and I could see that one of Tick's ears had been bitten and the side of his face was swollen up. I was about to put him on the leash when I heard Connie calling me from the window.

I thought that she was going to be angry because those dogs must have kept her up all night.

'I'm really sorry,' I said. 'He doesn't do this very often.'

'That's okay,' said Connie. 'Last night they got into a bit of a fight. We locked up Sheba so they couldn't get at her but you know what it's like. I hope he isn't hurt too badly.'

'If he is, it serves him right.'

'Would you like to come in?' she said. 'How about a cup of coffee?'

I was about to refuse and say that I should get Tick home and tie him up but then I realized I hadn't seen Connie for a long time.

'I'd love a cup of coffee,' I said, 'if it's not a problem.'

'Come on in,' she said.

I wouldn't say that Connie and I are close friends but I've always felt as though I know her a little better than the other women, since we were in language school together. She and I had the same tutors and neither of us was very good at Hindi.

We struggled together through the lessons and drilled each other with flash cards. For a while we made a pact that we would only speak in Hindi but that didn't last very long because both of us enjoy talking and there wasn't anything worse than trying to tell each other something very important with a vocabulary of only fifteen words.

Because I am from Minnesota and Connie's home is in Manitoba we thought of ourselves as coming from the same part of the world. Though I've never been to Canada, I remember one time my brother Earl went up to Winnipeg for a boy scout camp. It's odd how living so far away from home makes you realize there really isn't that much difference between Minnesota and Manitoba. It's just across the border.

I used to keep in touch with Connie much more regularly and during the first few years when I was in Ranchi and she was off in some village in the middle of nowhere with her husband, who was teaching tribals how to raise pigs, we wrote letters to each other. But after a while we grew apart. Connie didn't have children until quite a few years after I had mine and that may have been part of the reason I lost touch with her. I was so busy taking care of Tim and Michael. It's strange how people change when they have kids. Connie has a girl named Cynthia, who's in first grade. She's very pretty and always dressed up like a china doll. I think Connie must spend all her time dressing her up and doing her hair. She's like that, very fastidious about her own clothes too. When I see her with Cynthia I always wonder what I would have been like if I'd had a daughter. After they were eight or nine, Tim and Michael took care of themselves and I stopped trying to make them look neat or comb their hair. I would have liked to have a daughter, even though I'm very happy with my boys. I don't think I would have been like Connie, though, dressing her up in all those lacy things and putting ribbons in her hair. I would have liked a girl just because she wouldn't always track mud

46

into the house or leave her PE clothes lying in the living room. I'm not complaining about the boys but sometimes I wish they were a little more aware of the time I spend keeping the house in order. I think if I had a daughter, I'd be able to talk with her much more than I do with Tim and Michael, share things with her. I think I could be closer to a girl.

'Sometimes I wish a leopard would just take our dog,' I said, as Connie opened the door for me.

'When we got Sheba, Ted and I decided that we would get a female because she wouldn't wander off.'

'Sure. But then you get all the canine Romeos in your yard,' I said. 'That's just as bad.'

'As long as we keep her locked up, it's okay. I don't really mind. Last night our cook went out and threw a bucket of water on two of the dogs that got into a fight. I'm only worried that Sheba's going to sneak out and then we'll have puppies.'

'You haven't thought of getting her spayed?' I said.

'I have, but somehow it doesn't seem like a very nice thing to do,' said Connie, an embarrassed smile on her face. 'Besides, labradors have a way of getting so fat when they're spayed.'

I had to laugh, talking like this about the dogs, it seemed so matter of fact.

'Look at all of them sitting there with their tongues hanging out,' I said.

'I guess men are like that too,' said Connie.

It wasn't something I expected her to say; she is quite conservative about a lot of things.

'Do you think they enjoy mating, or is it just a kind of instinct for them?' she said, in a curious voice.

'I don't know. I've never discussed it with Tick,' I said.

Connie's cook brought in a tray of coffee which he put down on the table in front of us. Her house is a newer building than Murchison and more modern in many ways. Connie has decorated it in a kind of frilly, feminine style, with lace borders

47

on the curtains and little doilies everywhere. Her cushions are also fussy and the whole place has the feeling of a victorian doll house.

'What do you think, Rachel? Are people just like animals, I mean about sex?' she said.

'Maybe, in some ways,' I said. 'But it's not quite the same.'

'With men at least, it's such an instinct . . . such a heartless thing,' she said.

'Could be,' I said. 'I think we're different, certainly.'

It was strange talking like this with Connie after so many years. When we were together at the language school, both of us were newly married. We had a lot in common and our conversations would get quite personal sometimes. But now, after so many years had passed, I felt awkward talking with her and it surprised me that she would start right in, as if we were young brides fresh on the mission field.

'I was reading in a magazine that they took a poll in Canada and sixty percent of the women said they didn't feel like having sex more than once a week. On the other hand, eighty percent of the men wanted sex three times a week.'

'Can you imagine answering questions like that?' I said, trying to steer her off the subject.

'The same poll said that fifty percent of the men admitted that they were having extra-marital affairs and only twenty percent of the women.' Connie wasn't easily deflected.

'It's probably even higher in America,' I said.

'Can I ask you something?' said Connie, looking at me with her pert, uneasy face.

'What?' I said, joking, 'Do you want to know whether I want sex once or twice a week?'

'No, I was wondering whether you ever worry about Frank having an affair?' she said.

'I don't,' I said. 'He's not that kind of person.'

48

'Well I don't mean to suggest anything but they say it's always the person you least expect, who has an affair.'

'You've been reading too many magazines,' I said.

'A couple of years ago, magazines wouldn't even publish things like that,' said Connie. 'Nowadays, it's everywhere. That's all people in Canada seem to be thinking about. Sex.'

'It must be those long, cold winters,' I said.

'It's those long, hot summers in Gujarat that I worry about,' said Connie.

'Come on, Ted would never be unfaithful,' I said.

'I don't know,' she said. 'He's very innocent about some things and I don't think he's cheated on me yet. But if he got the chance, I think he would.'

'You shouldn't worry about it, Connie. As soon as you start doubting him, it only makes it worse.'

'I can't help it. When I'm away from him for so long, that's all I think about.'

'Well, who's he going to find in the middle of Gujarat?' I said.

'He's got a new extension worker in his field group,' said Connie, looking down. 'A real bright girl from Ahmedabad. She's just out of college and very pretty.'

'Nothing's going to happen,' I said.

'Maybe not. I can't help worrying, though. I just wish I was down there right now to keep an eye on him, but with Cynthia in school I have to stay up here. As it is she's missed a month already and they say that first grade is the most important year.'

'I really don't think you're being fair on Ted or on yourself. This woman isn't going to chase after him and he's certainly not the type to make a pass at her.'

'Oh Rachel, I'm sorry. I don't mean to burden you with this but it's just that I didn't have anyone to talk with and it's been worrying me a lot.'

49

'Well, why don't you write to Ted and tell him that you're concerned? Or make a joke of it. He'll get the hint.'

'I don't want to put ideas in his head,' said Connie.

'Now you're being silly. I think you should cancel your magazine subscriptions, forget about that extension worker, and put the whole thing out of your mind.'

'But I can't,' said Connie. 'All I do is sit in this house the whole day long and think about it happening and try to imagine what I'd do. I'd have to leave him, wouldn't I? And then where would I be? I've never had a job before. I don't have any skills. It's hard for a person without qualifications to get a job in Canada.'

'Good heavens,' I said, 'you've really worked yourself into a state. Before you even know for sure that Ted is having an affair, you're talking about leaving him.'

'Well I'm not like you. I can't trust my husband. I can't have him living five hundred miles away and know for sure that he's still mine. Oh Rachel, I'm so confused.'

Connie began to cry and I put my arm around her, trying to be comforting. She was shaking all over and I could tell it had been bothering her a lot and she needed to get it off her chest. I felt sorry for her but I also felt annoyed because she sounded so pathetic. I let her cry, and she bent down and held her hands to her face so that she was almost doubled up, sobbing as though she'd had the wind knocked out of her.

Just then the dogs got into a fight outside and there was a terrible snarling and barking. I could see that Tick was in the middle of it and there was nothing to do but leave Connie for a moment and try to break it up. I went outside and shouted at Tick, glad to be able to shout at someone. He and another dog had ganged up on a smaller, grey coloured mongrel and they looked as though they were going to kill it if I didn't stop them. My shouts and yells did nothing but the cook came out just then and he must have had a bucket ready for he went right up to the dogs and splashed it on them. Tick hates to get wet and he must have seen it coming because he let go just as the water hit them and it got him full in the face. With a yelp, he ran and hid under the windowboxes, turning into a coward all of a sudden.

When I went back inside, Connie was standing at the window. Even though her face was still streaked with tears, I could see that she had got control of herself again.

'I'm sorry Rachel,' she said. 'Don't mind me. I'm being silly.'

'You don't have to apologize to me. I just hate to see you get like this,' I said. 'Please don't dwell on it.'

'I'll try not to,' she said, putting on a brave face. 'I'm glad you came by.'

'I should take my mutt home,' I said, 'otherwise he's going to get into another fight.'

'Thank you for listening,' said Connie, kissing me on the cheek.

'Come by any time,' I said. 'We can practise our Hindi, if nothing else.'

She smiled and came to the door as I went out. Tick was still hiding under the windowboxes and crawled out cautiously, when I called him, knowing that he was in deep trouble. I put the leash on him and turned to wave to Connie. She gave a weak little wave and I felt terrible leaving her like that but there was nothing to be done. Tick had disgraced himself and Connie suspected her husband of having an affair. I didn't want to get caught in the middle.

I don't usually get depressed but after my conversation with Connie I felt so strange, lonely and uncertain. That night, while he was working on his homework, I asked Tim whether he thought I was happy or not. He gave me that quizzical, impatient look he gets when he doesn't quite understand what

51

I'm saying. Michael was in the bedroom working on his beetle collection.

'Sure, Mom. You're happy most of the time,' he said.

'Yes, of course,' I said, as if he'd reassured me. 'I've got two wonderful boys. Why shouldn't I be happy?'

'I haven't ever seen you cry, Mom. You know, right in the middle of biology, Mrs Edwards just started crying,' said Tim. 'It was so weird. We hadn't even been making a lot of noise.'

'I cry sometimes. Usually when I'm happy,' I said, but when I thought about it, the last time I cried was more than two years ago. Maybe there's something wrong with my tear ducts, I thought. It can't be healthy. You need to rinse your eyes out once in a while. Actually, I've never tried to hold back my feelings, not even in front of the boys, but somehow I've never been too emotional, not outwardly at least.

'Is something wrong?' said Tim, looking at me strangely.

'Nothing, I was just thinking.'

'Has Dad ever seen you cry?' asked Tim.

'Sure. Lots of times. When I first arrived in India, I cried a lot.'

'You didn't like it here?' he said.

'I was homesick, that's all,' I said. 'It wasn't that I didn't like it, just the thought of being so far away from my family used to make me sad.' I can talk with Tim in a way that I could never do with Frank or Michael. Frank is always too preoccupied and keeps giving me impatient looks when I try to explain what I am feeling. He's a psychiatrist but he isn't very good at listening to his wife. Michael — maybe he's too young to open up, but there's something else about him, a sort of restlessness. Tim is more sensitive and never really looks me in the eye, unlike Michael, who has such a direct and open stare. There's more of Frank in him as well and I know he misses his father all the time. Maybe I'm just

52

fooling myself and it's their age which makes me think they're different.

'Is it difficult for you, living away from your husband?' said Renuka.

'Yes, but sometimes I think I'm actually getting used to it,' I said. 'For the past eight years, I've spent more time away from Frank than I've been with him.'

'Does he hold it against you?' asked Renuka.

'I don't think so,' I said. 'He's very committed to his work.'

'You could always put the boys in boarding, couldn't you? At least for a couple of months,' said Renuka. 'They're old enough.'

'I've thought about that lots of times,' I said. 'I know there really isn't any reason for me to stay up here.'

But there was a reason; I don't know what to call it, an incident, a vision, an obscenity. There it was, as clear in my mind today as the moment I saw it happen, an act of cruelty and madness.

'There's something which I haven't told anyone before. It's very ugly. I haven't even told Frank. It's one of those things you keep inside yourself and it eats away at your mind.'

Renuka looked at me, surprised.

'Maybe you never grew up with the same concept of evil,' I said, 'but I was raised in a small town, near a lake which was so clean in those days that we could drink the water straight from the shore. The only mad person I knew about was an old hobo who lived by himself in a shack in the forest. We were never allowed to go near the place, but my brothers told me that he used to catch trout and hang them from the trees. We were simple farm people and we had never heard of psychiatrists and Freud, except as distant, unhealthy creatures. When I got a scholarship to study in Chicago it was a big thing, almost as big as coming out to India. That was where I met Frank, in college. He was almost finished with his degree. At first I was frightened of him. I thought he was going to hypnotize me in some dark alley, or make me lie on a couch and levitate. He used to laugh at me and tried to explain that psychology wasn't really all that wicked. My parents never understood, even though they accepted him for what he was. They still couldn't believe that their daughter would marry a man who dealt with the perversions of the human mind.

'If that had been true, I would never have agreed to be his wife. But soon after I met Frank, I realized that he was not an evil sorcerer. He was a Christian. There's no other way of saying it; a man who believed in human kindness and cared for people's sanity just as much as a doctor cares for a person's health. I knew that he was a good man. Why else would he have given up the chance of a steady practice in Chicago and come to India to work as a missionary? He didn't want to be a neighbourhood shrink, catering to every suburban neurosis. He wanted to work with people who really needed his care. That's why he came to Ranchi; that was why I came with him myself.

'When we first got there, I wanted to make myself useful and so I went around the wards, making sure that the sweepers and ayahs were doing their jobs. A lot of the work was done by the patients themselves. There was a young boy named Keshav. He was thin and unattractive but he dressed himself very neatly and would spend hours darning the holes in his shirt. I don't know what was wrong with Keshav. He was simple-minded, hardly able to speak, with a shuffle to his walk. I put him to work in the laundry and he would go about the home, collecting dirty sheets and linen to be washed each week. I also taught him how to make a bed and he would do it very carefully, so that there wasn't the slightest wrinkle on the sheet.

'There were two other patients named Chaman and Gopal, who were inseparable friends, except they hardly said anything to each other. I never saw them laugh together, or share a private joke. But they were always side by side and I thought of them as twins, even though they didn't look at all alike. We let them do odd jobs around the home and they had taken carpentry lessons and knew how to join a broken chair or fix a hinge. Chaman and Gopal had always seemed quite gentle to me and their faces had bewildered, childish expressions. They slept a lot, lying side by side in the shade of one of the neem trees on the compound with their heads cushioned on their arms.

'It was our first year in Ranchi and I was three months pregnant with Tim. For some reason I had gone to the laundry, which was located at the back of the compound, with several giant vats and an incinerator which heated water at the same time as burning trash. At first it didn't seem as though anyone was there. The doors were shut but in the home there are no locks or bolts as a precaution. When I opened the door to the room where the dirty linen was sorted into piles, I first saw Gopal. He had his back to me and I could see that he was struggling with something on the ground. There was a cupboard which blocked my view but as I took a step forward, I saw what was happening. Keshav was crouched on the floor and Gopal was holding him by the back of the neck. Chaman was on the other side. He had one arm around Keshav's waist and he was moving his whole body with a kind of broken, frantic rhythm. I knew that Keshav was being raped. I could hear him whimpering. Chaman and Gopal were so absorbed in what they were doing, neither of them saw me standing there. I was about to shout but something came over me and I couldn't make a sound. They were like animals. Slowly I backed away to the door and ran towards our house. There was no one else nearby.

'I have never been so terrified in all my life. Just the sight of them was so obscene, so hideous. Frank was not at home.

55

He had gone into town. When I got inside our bungalow, I locked the bedroom door and lay there for a long time, trying to forget, trying to erase what I had seen, but nothing could take it away. It made me hate the place. For the first time, I knew what terror meant. The fear of having witnessed something so brutal and the feeling of being mute and helpless. I felt as though I had been part of that obscenity, an accomplice to the act.

'When Frank came back for lunch, I had planned to tell him what I had seen but somehow I couldn't bring myself to describe those men and the sight of Keshav kneeling on the floor. It was impossible to explain the look on Chaman's face, so innocent and yet so menacing. Frank could sense that I was upset, though I tried to hide it. He asked me several times if I was okay but I said that it was just my nausea coming on again. With Tim, I had a lot of morning sickness.

'It was two days before I could get myself to go outside again. As I went across to the kitchens, Chaman and Gopal were lying under one of the trees, fast asleep. I turned the corner of the main building and saw Keshav, carrying an armload of dish towels towards the laundry. I ran up to him and touched his shoulder. He turned and looked at me with dull, sad eyes, not comprehending my concern. More than anything, Keshav was the one who frightened me; he was unchanged, expressionless and what I'd seen might never have happened if I hadn't looked into that room.'

CHAPTER 5

POT ROAST	**Bindal Chand**
1/2 cup oil	1/2 teaspoon black pepper
4 lbs. mutton or pork	1/2 teaspoon dried mustard
4 onions chopped fine	1/2 teaspoon paprika
1 cup mushrooms, sliced	1 tablespoon salt
4 carrots, diced	3 sprigs parsley
5 tomatoes, chopped	flour to thicken gravy
6 potatoes, halved	1 cup cold water

Heat oil in a heavy pot or pressure cooker, then thoroughly brown the meat on all sides. Remove meat to platter. Put onions, mushrooms, carrots and tomatoes into the pot and stir till browned. Replace meat and sprinkle salt, pepper, mustard and paprika over it. Add 1 cup of water and cover tightly. Cook very slowly on low flame. Turn meat over once while cooking for four to five hours. About an hour before serving, lay potatoes on top of meat to steam. When all is tender, remove meat to hot platter and surround with potatoes. Garnish with parsley. Add enough water to the gravy to make desired amount and thicken with flour. Use a pressure cooker to reduce cooking time and save fuel.

I have a cook, like everyone else on the hillside. His name is Bindal Chand but we call him Bindru. He is a hillman and comes from a village about thirty miles away. Even though I've been in India twelve years, it's still not something I can get used to — servants. Whenever we go back to the States on furlough and I say something about the cook or the sweeper, women smirk at me and look away, as though I'm spoiled. They don't realize how much trouble servants can be. Sometimes I think it's more work having a cook. I have to watch him all the time to make sure he keeps the kitchen clean and boils the drinking water. If I want something cooked a special way, I have to explain it to him several times until he understands. Bindru is a good cook but he does things the way he's always done them and it's hard to get him to change. It took me two years to get him to stop putting turnips in the pot roast, because the boys hate turnips and I'm not particularly fond of them myself. And then of course, he has his own problems and I am always worrying about his family back in the village. In an American kitchen, you've got conveniences, dish washers, toaster ovens and food processors. You push a button and your work is done. But with a cook you have to explain it all so carefully.

Some women, like Esther Rainey, just leave their cooks alone to run the kitchen. They don't even make a cup of coffee for themselves. I'm not like that. I enjoy cooking and being in the kitchen. Bindru probably gets fed up with me, because I'm always getting in his way and tasting what he's made and asking why something's finished and I wasn't told about it. He's very patient but I know sometimes he wishes that the memsahib would just leave him alone.

We "inherited" Bindru from the Jacksons. They were an old missionary couple who retired the same year we came to India. Mrs Jackson was a real meat and potatoes woman and Bindru's specialty is pot roast. I had to break him of the habit after Frank started putting on weight. Bindru's idea of vegetables was mashed potatoes.

Bindru must be over seventy, even though he claims to be forty-one. He wears dentures and dyes his hair. He always has some ache or pain and his eyes are constantly watering as though he's been cutting onions. I keep thinking that we should let him retire but I know that he has to support his family. Bindru has three daughters and he's still paying off the loans he took to get them married. His wife lives in the village and they have some land which he says his creditors are trying to take away from him. I just don't have the heart to make him retire. One time I mentioned it and he looked so miserable I never brought it up again, even though he's getting so old, he can hardly do the work. Of course it's nice to have someone who will wash the dishes and cook up Tick's food, the tripe and bones which we buy from the meat wallah. The boys like Bindru too, and he'll do anything they say. They tease me because of the way I talk to Bindru, with my 'kitchen Hindi', but I ignore them. I didn't grow up in India like them and I've never been very good with languages.

I think the boys are happy on the hillside and even though they talk about going back to America, they probably wouldn't like it there. Tim and Michael are fond of their teachers and I think they get a pretty good education at the school. In some ways the hillside is a very isolated place and I worry about what will happen to them when they leave and go out into the world, but at the same time they have their friends and it's a healthy place for them to be, which is probably more important at this age.

At one time, I thought of teaching at the school. They even offered me a job but I didn't think it would be fair on the boys having to put up with their mother in the classroom as well as at home. Frank thought it was a good idea, but I somehow couldn't see myself standing in front of a blackboard every day. Besides, I have no qualifications.

I've been den mother for the cub scouts these last three years and that's the sort of thing I can enjoy. Once a month, I let the boys invite a friend out of boarding for the weekend and make a special batch of cookies or fudge on Sunday afternoon. I'm quite busy being a mother so that I don't really need another job.

Renuka is the one who encouraged me to become editor of the cookbook. Last year when they announced at the Women's Club that they were looking for volunteers, Esther Rainey approached me after the meeting. She said a lot of women were willing to help on the committee but nobody wanted to be the editor. They were looking for someone who would be staying on the hillside for most of the year. I didn't really think that I could do it but Renuka was convinced that it was just the kind of work that I'd enjoy. She wouldn't leave me alone until I agreed to take the job. When I started I didn't know how I'd be able to manage. I knew it would be a lot of work and I really wanted to do it properly if I was going to do it at all.

Working at home is difficult because of all the interruptions, the wallahs coming to the door, the coolies bringing notes from Esther Rainey asking for one thing or another, visitors dropping by for a cup of coffee. Several times I've had to lock myself into the bedroom just to get anything done. All of the recipes have to be sorted and filed. I have to make copies and pass them around to each of the women on the committee so that they can try them out. Meanwhile, I have to write the introduction, find a reliable printer and explain fifteen times to Mary Bettman that the illustrations have to be done in pen and ink, not water colour.

So many women talk about starting their own careers but really I don't feel dissatisfied being a mother and a housewife. I wouldn't want a full time job. I like to work at home, make the beds, clean up after the boys. The only part I don't enjoy is washing clothes and for that I have a dhobi who takes the laundry once a week and brings it back all neatly ironed and smelling of woodsmoke.

Every Thursday he squats down on the bedroom carpet and counts the dirty clothes. I write them down in my dhobi book and check to make sure he's brought back all the clothes he took last week. He carries them away on his back, wrapped up in a sheet, bent double under the weight of all that laundry. The dhobi reminds me of one of those characters from *Pilgrim's Progress*, carrying a burden of sins on his shoulders.

I never liked that book. The boys have a special edition which one of my aunts gave them. I used to read it aloud to them but there was something annoying about Mr Goodfellow and the heavenly gates, a kind of simplistic morality which is so much a part of the hillside.

Last Sunday Rev Turner's sermon was about the 'Recipes of Faith'. He began by talking about the different ingredients of Christian witness, how you needed a cup of humour, a pound of patience and three heaped tablespoons of honesty. It was a bad sermon and not too many people laughed. I began to feel self-conscious since Rev Turner kept looking at me and belabouring the point until I thought he was going to ask me to whip up the recipe right there in front of everybody and show them how honest and upright I could be. He finally ended by saying that the Bible was God's cookbook and we just had to follow the recipes of faith.

Rev Turner is not the most inspiring preacher and he usually comes up with some of the worst sermons I've ever heard. He's also very prejudiced in his views. A couple of years ago, Frank had an argument with him about psychiatry. I don't know how it started but they both got quite worked up and in the end Frank called him a bigot. Rev Turner said that psychology was an evil science and implied that Frank could not possibly be a good Christian if he believed in Freudian analysis. Frank asked if Rev Turner had ever read Freud and he said he hadn't 'cared to', which was when the two of them started arguing in earnest.

It was after a P.T.A. meeting at the school and we were having coffee and doughnuts. I got worried because Frank was getting angry and Rev Turner had that smug, self-righteous look on his face. He told Frank that the only cure for a 'lunatic' was the 'healing spirit of God'. According to him, anyone who was 'a mental case' was possessed by the devil and no human powers of reasoning could possibly help that person, only the 'love of our Lord Jesus Christ'. He told Frank about some old tramp he'd known in Arkansas, where he had his first church, who was 'completely off his rocker'. The tramp had been to several institutions and nothing had worked until he walked into the church one Sunday morning and stumbled up the aisle. Rev Turner stopped the service. He laid his hands on the man and prayed. The next day the tramp was fine, 'absolutely sane', and he became the most devout member of the church.

Frank said that he didn't doubt the powers of the holy spirit but there were a lot of times when modern methods of psycho-analysis could do a lot of good. He also said he didn't feel it was exactly Christian of Rev Turner to call someone a lunatic.

Their voices grew so loud that a lot of people turned around to hear what was going on. I finally grabbed Frank's arm and said that we should be heading home. I was afraid that he would say something really terrible. Fortunately, the next day he had to leave for Ranchi and the whole thing blew over.

It's strange but I don't miss Frank all that much any more. He used to come up to the hillside more frequently when the boys were younger but now it's only once or twice a year. He came up in the middle of May this year for a little over a week. I used to get so angry with Frank, furious because we had to live apart, but somehow I'm more complacent now. It doesn't bother me the way it did before. I worry about him sometimes because I know he doesn't get enough sleep in Ranchi. It's so hot for one thing and the mosquitoes are terrible. He drives himself so hard, even when we're down there during the holidays. Right now he's in the middle of building a new outpatients' centre at the home and he has to spend a lot of time making sure the contractors are doing their work correctly and keeping to the schedule. His assistant, Mr Abraham, could probably do it all but Frank likes to supervise everything himself. That's why he works so hard. I wish that he would ease up a little and take better care of himself. One of the cooks at the home makes his meals for him but I know Frank doesn't eat properly and when he was here in May, I could see he'd lost some weight. I know it's hard on him being alone down there but I guess it's the work that keeps him going, those long hours at night when he does his correspondence. I keep telling him that he should hire a secretary but the home is so short on staff, Frank says he'd rather hire another nurse, if they could afford one.

I feel guilty about abandoning him and coming up to the hillside but I know that it would be much worse if I was down there with him. I'd have so little to do and I'd be irritable all the time. I sometimes wonder if I still love him. It's not something I like to think about but it seems as though our marriage has become a kind of hollow convention which we uphold without any emotional ties. That isn't really true because whenever Frank comes up to the hillside, I do look forward to having him here. But when he's down in Ranchi, sometimes I forget I've even got a husband.

That first year, when we were in language school and staying at Kisli Lodge, it was so different. We'd go for long walks and practise our Hindi vocabulary while having a picnic at the stream, or else we would go down to the bazaar and wander around the second-hand shops. Frank has never been a very outgoing person but he was fun to be with in those days. Maybe I'm just being too idealistic and the first years of marriage are never the same as later on. We used to talk about so many things together, books we'd read or movies we'd seen. I've always loved movies and we used to go down to the Odeon theatre every weekend to see the English pictures. We saw so many good movies, *Beckett, Bridge on the River Kwai,* and a lot of westerns which Frank enjoyed. It was fun to be with him and he would groan whenever John Wayne saved the day. The Odeon used to have box seats in the back with moth-eaten velvet curtains. Sometimes the projectionist would get the reels mixed up or the lights would go off and we would sit for half an hour in darkness, eating peanuts which we bought from the old woman who sits outside the Odeon. We would hold hands as we sat there in the dark with that silver tunnel of light flickering onto the screen. I would cry at the sad parts and Frank would laugh to see me sniffling away at some stupid love story. He never got emotional even in the most tragic movies.

A couple of times we even went to a Hindi movie with one of the tutors from the language school. It was a lot of fun, though I didn't speak enough of the language to understand very much. One of the films was a historical movie set during the Mughal period. It was very melodramatic, with all of these soldiers dressed in what looked like Roman costumes. There was a scene in which a man was supposed to be crushed to death by an elephant and it was so unbelievable that I started to giggle and I was the only person in the cinema hall who was laughing because all of this blood was squirting out of the man and you could tell the elephant wasn't stamping on him at all.

That first year on the hillside spoiled me. As soon as we went down to Ranchi, I was so disappointed in our bungalow and all of the depressing things about the home. Frank also seemed to change. Up in the hills he didn't have very much to do but running the mental home was a big responsibility for him and he took it very seriously. At first it wasn't so bad but

64

I sometimes felt as though I was getting in his way. He would get preoccupied with all of the problems at the home and the paperwork which never seemed to end. There would always be some sort of crisis. One of the patients would try to kill themselves or there would be a fight or the tube well would break down.

We hadn't planned to have children for several years but I wasn't very careful and got pregnant during our second month in Ranchi. Frank was worried when I told him, but in some ways I was happy. There was nothing much for me to do and I looked forward to being a mother. Since the baby would arrive in June, we decided to come up to the hillside and have the delivery here. The hospital in Ranchi wasn't very good and I didn't like the idea of looking after a newborn baby in that heat. We came up about a month ahead of time and I got a room at Kisli Lodge. Frank went back down to Ranchi for a couple of weeks and then returned for the delivery.

Tim was born on the 8th of June, just around midnight. My contractions had started in the afternoon and instead of getting a dandie I decided to walk. Frank was with me and every time I'd get a contraction, we would stop and I'd put my head on his shoulder until it subsided. The whole thing wasn't as painful as I had expected. Halfway down the path, we happened to meet Mrs Francis Mitchum. She was coming back from the hospital and we didn't tell her that I was in labour. Mrs Mitchum started chatting and she could go on for quite a while. I don't know what it is, but some women always feel the need to boast about their own deliveries and describe the gruesome details. Mrs Mitchum was telling me that she had thirty-six hours labour in a tent in the middle of Madhya Pradesh, without mosquito nets, and her husband thought she was going to die. At that point I began to feel another contraction coming on and I closed my eyes and leaned on Frank. Mrs Mitchum stopped abruptly.

'Goodness,' she said, 'What's happening?'

I started to laugh, she sounded so alarmed. Frank told her that I was in labour.

'Well, what are you doing here?' she said. 'Get her to the hospital right away.'

'That's where we're going,' said Frank.

Afterwards when she came to visit me and brought a pair of woollen booties for Tim, Mrs Mitchum scolded me for being so irresponsible.

'You could have had him right there on the path,' she said. 'What if a coolie had come along?'

I stayed on the hillside until October while Frank went back and forth to Ranchi. I missed him when he was away but I was so busy taking care of Tim, I didn't feel so lonely.

When Renuka heard that Frank was coming up for a visit in May, she told me that she was interested in meeting him.

'I've never spoken to a psychiatrist before,' she said. 'What is he like?'

'He's quiet, a little serious,' I said. 'Actually, you'd never guess he was a psychiatrist if you met him.'

'What do you mean?' said Renuka.

'Well, he doesn't give you the impression of being the sort of person who pokes about in people's minds.'

'Is he very religious?' said Renuka.

'In his own way, yes,' I said.

'Does he confide in you about his patients? Does he tell you what they talk about?' she asked.

'Not very often,' I said. 'And I don't usually ask.'

'Don't you get curious sometimes?' said Renuka.

'Before we got married, when Frank was still doing his internship, he used to tell me about some of the cases he was handling, and we would discuss them in a general sort of way. But usually, it wasn't all that interesting. I guess, when you get down to it, personal problems are really only interesting for the persons themselves. Most of it was pretty boring. The patients he has now are different, really. They're much more serious cases. Sometimes they're not able to tell him very much.'

'I've always wanted to consult with a psychiatrist,' said Renuka, 'but the one man whom I heard about in Calcutta, a Dr Basu, was such a lecher, I wouldn't have gone within a hundred feet of him.'

'But why would you want to see a psychiatrist?' I said.

Renuka gave me a mysterious look.

'When I was at St Mary's in Darjeeling, all of the catholic girls used to go to confession and I would get so jealous of them. Father Amos, an old Italian priest, used to come to school twice a week and he would go into the confessional and the catholic girls would line up outside the door. The nuns would let them in one at a time. Those of us that weren't Christians didn't have to go to confession. I resented that and somehow I felt as though I was being cheated. It was something I wanted to do; I wanted to confess my sins to Father Amos.'

'Did you really have that much to confess?' I said.

'You'd never imagine what a wicked girl I was,' said Renuka. 'Such impure thoughts.'

I had always tried to imagine Renuka as a schoolgirl, with pig-tails and a pleated skirt. It was so hard to picture her like that and yet at times she had a very childlike face and the way she spoke, I could hear a youthful mischief in her voice.

Frank got to Murchison in the evening, just at dusk. The boys and I had been waiting all day for him but his train had been delayed and he arrived exhausted. I was surprised how old he looked. It was so good to see him after almost three months.

The boys were eager to show him all the things that they'd been doing but Frank looked so tired, I told them to wait until tomorrow. Bindru had made a special dinner but I noticed that Frank didn't eat very much. He said that the heat had been terrible and the fans in his compartment on the train hadn't been working. After dinner, he went straight to bed.

It was only the next morning that I got a chance to talk with him. The boys had gone to school and we took our coffee out to the verandah.

'How long are you going to stay this time?' I said.

Frank looked at me and frowned.

'A week and a half,' he said.

'That's all?' I said.

'Rachel, the auditors are coming on the 28th and the accounts are such a mess.'

'Well, at least you're not going down tomorrow,' I said.

'I'm sorry,' he said, touching my hand.

'It's okay,' I said. 'I didn't mean to start off like this. It's just, sometimes I wish you could stay a while.'

'Maybe in October,' he said.

'Maybe,' I said, knowing it would never happen.

'So, how are things?' he said.

'All right,' I said. 'I want you to meet a friend of mine, Renuka Sen. She's coming to dinner tomorrow night.'

'You mentioned her in one of your letters,' he said. 'She's the one who writes poetry?'

I nodded.

'Is she Bengali?'

'Yes,' I said.

There was so much I wanted to tell Frank about Renuka but I didn't know where to begin.

'She's a terrific Scrabble player,' I said.

'Maybe I can challenge her,' he said.

Frank used to be quite good.

'You better be careful,' I said. 'She might just beat you.'

I had been a little nervous about inviting Renuka over because I wasn't quite sure how she'd react to Frank. He has a way of being a bit reserved with people whom he's never met before. But they seemed to get along quite well. Renuka arrived a little late. She was dressed in a silk sari and even had some lipstick on. As usual she'd brought flowers, a spray of baby's breath and two tiger lilies. She'd also found a porcupine quill along the path which she gave Michael to add to his collection.

After I had introduced Renuka to Frank, I had to go into the kitchen and see how dinner was coming along. The boys were with them and I could hear Renuka asking Tim about an art project he had done. She had loaned him one of her miniature paintings to copy and he did a pretty good job of it, though I was terrified the painting might get ruined.

As we sat down at the table, Renuka started to ask Frank about his work. He seemed a little reluctant to discuss his patients but gradually opened up. He told Renuka about a local politician in Ranchi who had tried to get his wife admitted to the home. As it turned out, the woman was perfectly sane and the husband just wanted to get rid of her because he was having an affair.

'What's an affair?' said Michael.

I looked at Frank, as if to say, 'it serves you right'. Tim was staring at his plate and blushing because I guess he knew. Before either of us could answer, Renuka turned to Michael who was sitting beside her and whispered in his ear. I couldn't hear what she said but Michael started to laugh.

'You know, we have a history of madness in our family,' said Renuka. 'Have I ever told you, Rachel, about my grandfather who sold half his property for a bottle of rosewater sharbat which was supposed to have been made for Suraj ud Daowla, the Nawab of Bengal? He hoped it would restore his virility but when the bottle was uncorked there was such a stink that the windows had to be left open for three weeks.'

'I'm sure you're making that up,' I said.

'Absolutely not,' said Renuka. 'Our family is full of crazy people. You see, we're quite inbred. Our ancestral home used to be in what is now Assam, near Cooch Behar. Though we were a family of wealthy landlords most Bengalis considered us a little wild and uncivilized so that the only people who would marry us were our own cousins. It led to a lot of unusual mutations. An uncle of mine is infamous for having dressed himself as a monkey and danced half-naked on Howrah bridge.'

Frank doesn't usually like people to make jokes about that sort of thing but he laughed as hard as all of us. After dinner, I had to bribe the boys with an extra piece of dessert to get them into bed.

'Rachel told me that you're a Scrabble player,' Frank said to Renuka, after we had moved into the living room again.

'Actually, I never played the game until this year. I must say I enjoy it very much,' she said.

'Would you like to play?' I said.

'Why not?' said Frank.

After we had set things up, I began to wish I hadn't suggested Scrabble. I had forgotten how competitive Frank can be. He doesn't like to lose at anything. The evening had started out so well and I was worried that the game might turn into a disaster. Renuka frowned as she picked up her tiles and put them carefully in order. She and I usually play with the boys and we never take it very seriously. We even let Michael cheat a little. Tonight there were just the three of us.

The game started off all right and I tried to keep the mood lighthearted by making silly mistakes. I mis-spelled raccoon

70

and Frank seemed to get annoyed. When Renuka put down "honour" he said he wasn't sure about "these British spellings" and I was worried that they might get into an argument. It seemed so stupid to let a game become like that but even Renuka was getting impatient and on edge. Frank won the first game by a point or two and I suggested that we stop but they wanted to play the best of three.

After the second game, which Renuka won, I told them I wasn't going to play any more. It was almost ten o'clock.

'Come on Rachel, you're going to win this time,' said Renuka.

'The two of you are much too good and much too serious for me,' I said.

'No. No. You have to play,' said Frank. 'No chickening out.'

I finally relented and somehow in this game, I seemed to be doing much better. I was getting all the best tiles and by some fluke I kept making double and triple word scores. It looked as though I might actually win. Frank was doing terribly but since I was winning, he didn't seem to mind so much. Renuka was about ten points behind when all the tiles ran out. She was able to use up four by spelling KNAVE. I was already down to four tiles, an L, a V, an A and a U. It didn't look as though I'd be able to make a word with all of them and the V was going to count four points against me if I didn't use it. For a few minutes, I just stared at the board and my mind went blank. Then suddenly I noticed the V in KNAVE and I realized that I could win. There was even a triple letter score, but I hesitated for a moment. Frank was watching me and I wondered if he'd be shocked. Very slowly, I set the letters down. The V which was already there came first and then the U, the L, the second V and finally the A. As I put it down, I looked at Frank. He was on the opposite side of the board and it took him a moment to figure it out.

71

'Rachel!' he said, his voice like Michael's when he gets surprised.

Renuka clapped her hands and then we all broke down in laughter. After that, it didn't matter who had won or lost.

CHAPTER 6

COCONUT COOKIES   **Jo Tyson**

1 cup sugar	1 tsp. soda
1 cup sour cream	1/2 tsp. salt
1 egg	1/2 cup coconut (grated)
2 cups flour	1 tsp. vanilla

Add sugar to cream: add beaten egg. Add sifted dry ingredients, then vanilla and grated coconut. Drop by spoonfuls on greased baking sheet and bake at 375 F. for 10–15 minutes. Makes 48.

Tuesday morning I had been at school, checking with Michael's teacher about a book which he had lost. As I was walking home, I heard someone calling out my name. Turning around, I saw Jo Tyson coming after me, looking very pregnant in a blue, tent-like dress. I hardly know her but we greeted each other like long-lost friends and I asked her how she was feeling.

'Much better now,' she said, a little out of breath. 'I think I'm over my morning sickness. Here, this is for the cookbook.'

She gave me the recipe card which she was holding.

'You know, it's weird but I never liked coconut until I got pregnant,' said Jo, 'and now I can't stop eating the stuff.'

'Thank you,' I said. 'We don't have many cookie recipes yet.'

'That's one my mother sent me. I tried them out and they were great.'

Jo Tyson always makes me feel uneasy. She's one of those younger missionary ladies who come out for just a year or two and still have that fresh, untrampled look about them. Their clothes are perma-press and fashionable. They cut their hair short and wear a lot of make-up on their eyes. It's strange, but I always feel out of place with them, maybe just because I'm older. They look like the models in Sears and Roebuck catalogues. I can't help but get annoyed by their chirpy optimism and the naïve way they look at India.

Jo and her husband are with the E.M.F., the Evangelical Missionary Fellowship, which is made up of several different fundamentalist denominations. Al Tyson is the head of the E.M.F. in India and has his office in New Delhi. He's a handsome, cowboy type who always grins at you as though he's showing off his teeth. He comes uphill quite often and drives around on a motorcycle. Jo is expecting their first child.

'I wanted to have a word with you,' she said, as we started up the path. 'You're friends with that Indian lady aren't you? The one who lives at Erinfell.'

'You mean Renuka Sen,' I said.

'I didn't know her name,' said Jo. 'Is she a Hindu or a Muslim?'

'She's a Hindu,' I said.

Jo shook her head.

'I just can't understand how someone could actually believe that they're going to be reborn as a frog or a cow or a bird,' she said.

'I'm sure it's not quite as simple as that,' I said, trying to put her in her place. But Jo wasn't even listening.

'Well, we were thinking, here she is living amongst us and nobody has shared the good news with her.'

74

'What good news?' I said, and then almost bit my tongue, realizing what she meant.

'The Christian message,' said Jo. 'Sometimes we seem to forget that God has sent us here to be his witnesses.'

'You mean, you want to convert Renuka?' I said, trying not to smile.

'Well, we thought it might be nice if we invited her to one of our prayer meetings next week,' said Jo.

'I really don't think that she'd be interested,' I said.

'I'm sure if you asked her, she might come along. All of us would like to get to know her better. And I'll tell you what. I'll make those coconut cookies so you can taste them.'

'Jo, I don't mean to sound rude, but I don't think Renuka would want to come to your meeting.'

'But as her friend, Rachel, doesn't it worry you that she hasn't accepted Jesus into her life?'

'No, I don't think that's any of my business.' I stopped short of adding, ' . . . or yours.'

Jo looked at me with a hurt expression, pausing a moment to catch her breath.

'I was talking with Ruth Dupree the other day,' said Jo. 'Both of us think that someone should witness to her. That's what we're here for, isn't it?'

'I really don't think it would be a good idea,' I said, trying to hold back my anger. Jo gave me a sour look, as if I was being unreasonable.

'E.M.F. is buying Erinfell from the Baptists, you know,' said Jo, 'and there are a lot of people in our mission who don't think it's right to be renting one of our houses to a non-Christian.'

'Is that a threat?' I said. 'You want me to tell Renuka that she has to become a Christian if she wants to keep on living here?'

'That's not what I meant at all,' said Jo.

'Well, that's certainly what it sounded like,' I said.

75

Jo was getting very red in the face, not just from the climb. I couldn't believe that anyone would talk like this. It seemed so petty and small-minded.

'Rachel, I think you have a duty as a Christian and a friend to share God's word with her.'

'And I think that she has a right to believe or not believe in whatever she wants,' I said. 'I'm not going to preach to her and I certainly don't think you have any right to do that either.'

'Well, I'm sorry you feel that way,' said Jo, stopping where the path forked left, towards her house. She looked so large and foolish, I just wanted to push her off the side of the hill and let her roll all the way to the bottom. I knew that if I stayed there any longer, I was going to really lose my temper so I turned away and carried on towards Murchison, still holding the recipe card which Jo had given me and resisting the urge to tear it up and throw the pieces down the khud.

I've always been a little wary of the E.M.F. because of their style and the way they talk. There's a kind of false piety about them that really gets on my nerves and they're always talking about money, how much is coming in and how much is being spent. They also seem to get all kinds of equipment into the country, new Landrovers and video cameras, computers and televisions.

The E.M.F. ladies have prayer meetings every week and I always get invited though I never go. Many of them are charismatics and they start speaking in tongues. That sort of thing embarrasses me. I guess I just like a quiet church and organ on a Sunday morning, nothing ecstatic or too emotional. My family were religious but never in a showy way. We used to worship every Sunday in the little church outside of Hopkins. There were mostly farmers there, sturdy

Swedes and Norsemen who never prayed out loud or spoke in tongues.

I pray sometimes when I'm alone because it makes me feel good afterwards, not because I'm pious or that I want forgiveness but just because I need to speak with someone when Frank's not here.

A few weeks ago, Al Tyson was on the hillside and preached in church. He is a large, imposing man with a salt and pepper beard. He looks a lot like a country-western singer, maybe because of the silver buckle on his belt or his plaid shirts. He delivered his sermon in a rich, southern baritone. I think he comes from Louisiana. I liked his accent but what he had to say was kind of disturbing. He talked about the "Calling of a Missionary" and he said how we must never forget that our real purpose was to "lead people to the Lord Jesus Christ". He said that a lot of missionaries were involved in other kinds of work, agriculture, education, medicine, administration, social work. These were good and valuable jobs for us to do, but foremost in our minds should be our willingness to, "spread the message of our Lord and bring converts to his altar". He said that evangelism was the highest goal of any Christian and he felt that those missionaries who shirked in that role, "are not being true to their calling". He said that each of us had been "summoned across the ocean" to minister amongst the disbelievers and the Lord expected us to be his evangelists. If we did not actively and aggressively seek to convert those Hindus and Muslims whom we met each day, then we were not fulfilling our mission and there was no reason for us to be here in India at all. According to him, if we were doctors then we must not only heal our patients physically but heal their spiritual wounds as well; if we were teachers then we must not only educate our students but persuade them to accept Christ into their hearts; if we worked with farmers then we must do more than just help

77

them improve their crops but also "sow in them the seeds of the Lord".

I know that a lot of people agreed with what he was saying and there are only a few of us on the hillside who believe in a different kind of "calling". To me it has always seemed that the most important thing about being a missionary is to live a Christian life, simply as an example for others. I would never try to convert somebody. I know that Frank feels the same way. He has his work to do and he does it because he believes that it is important and necessary, but he does not proselytize or try to make his patients accept Christianity. There is a chapel at the mental home and there are services each Sunday, but the patients are not forced to accept Christianity. I don't know, maybe we're wrong, maybe it is illogical to be a missionary who doesn't believe in evangelism, who doesn't go out and baptize the heathens. It is so hard to argue with the simple, uncomplicated faith of a man like Al Tyson. For him the world is black and white, Christian and non-Christian, and for a missionary like him, it must be the most important thing in the world to 'save a soul for Christ'. To me it seems so false, so full of prejudice and inconsistency, as though God is keeping a tally sheet on each of us and our faith will be measured by the number of converts we round up.

At one of our recent cookbook committee meetings, Midge Thompson, who is also with the E.M.F., was telling us about a young muslim man in the village where she and her husband work who used to disrupt their church services and make life difficult for them. Her husband prayed for him and finally confronted him one day and asked him to accept the Lord. She said that suddenly this change came over the man and he fell down and touched her husband's feet and asked for forgiveness. They took him into the church and laid their hands on him and prayed and the man asked to be baptized that same day. All of the other women were very impressed and kept cooing and nodding as she told the story but I just couldn't stand it and I had to say something. I told Midge that I was sure the man had gone through a spiritual experience but I didn't think it was right to expect God always to act in such a dramatic way. Of course, this made them all turn cold and they didn't want to discuss it with me. I think they look at me as someone who doesn't quite measure up to their standards.

That's part of the reason they don't like the idea of my friendship with Renuka, because I have never tried to turn her into a Christian. They can't understand why I accept her for what she is.

The E.M.F. gets most of its money from a television evangelist named Arthur Williams. I had never heard of him before but I guess he must be a household name in some parts of the United States. He came to the hillside last year, part of a 'world crusade' visiting all of the countries where his money was being distributed. Jo Tyson and her husband organized his visit to the hillside and they arranged to hold a 'prayer-service' at the school. Everybody was invited and we were told that the whole thing was going to be filmed for his television show. Of course I didn't want anything to do with it but when Renuka heard what was happening, she said she wanted to attend, just out of curiosity. I tried to tell her that it would be a mistake but she was absolutely determined.

'Don't worry, Rachel, I won't embarrass you,' she said.

'But it's going to be so awful,' I said. 'You don't know how crass these people can be.'

'That's why I want to go,' she said. 'I've always wanted to see what Arthur Williams was all about.'

'You've actually heard of him?' I said.

'Of course. He's famous, Rachel. I've read about him in *Time* magazine. He's supposed to be very convincing.'

'I'm sure he's just another fraud.'

'Perhaps, but at least it will be entertaining,' said Renuka.

'I'm not going,' I said.

'Please, Rachel. I wouldn't dare to go on my own. If you're there with me I won't feel so conspicuous.'

In the end, Renuka got her way and I found myself sitting in the gymnasium at the school. They had decided to hold the service there instead of in the chapel because there was more room. We got seats at the back of the bleachers. One end of the gym was set up like a stage with an electric organ and speakers. It looked more like the setting for a rock concert than for a religious service, except that behind the stage they had hung a colourful banner with a picture of a fish and a cross, combined in a stylized pattern. Somebody had also put a lectern in one corner of the stage with a Bible and a vase of blue hydrangeas. On either side, there were two men in suits, with television cameras and I wondered how they carried all this equipment around with them. Someone had mentioned that Arthur Williams had his own airplane but I didn't believe that. Renuka kept asking me questions which I couldn't answer — whether there would be communion, or if we were going to have to sing a hymn. I felt annoyed by her excitement. To her it was a kind of entertainment but for me it was an obscenity. Michael and Tim were sitting next to us and they too seemed absorbed by the array of lights and microphones which had sprouted all over the gym.

Finally Mr Burley, the school principal, appeared and welcomed us. He began by saying how fortunate we were to have Arthur Williams with us this evening and how he and his group had fit their visit in on a very tight schedule. They had just come from Africa and they were on their way to Thailand and Australia but the Lord had made it possible for them to come up here and share their message with all of us. He went on for a bit and then with a shy little shuffle of his feet, as though he himself was caught up in the dramatics of the evening, he held out his hands and welcomed Arthur Williams.

The spotlight wavered and through the door of the gym came a small, wiry man who seemed to have springs on the soles of his feet and was wearing a glittering jumpsuit with a large white bow tie. Renuka stifled a giggle as he leaped up onto the stage and took a microphone in his hand. It was hard to tell whether his hair was white or blonde, sort of vanilla coloured. He had a smooth, expressive face and a kind of youthful swagger that made him seem ageless. Everybody clapped as he made a bow and thanked us for our welcome. It seemed so unreal to be sitting there and watching this in the same gym where I had watched Tim and Michael playing basketball the week before and where we always held our barter sales. It was as though we had been transported all the way around the globe to some place in America.

Arthur Williams began with a prayer which was unlike any other prayer that I had heard before, even though everyone bowed their heads. He seemed to be on a first name basis with Jesus (he pronounced it Geee-zuss) and carried on a one way conversation which was meant to convince everyone in the audience that he was speaking to the Lord. It was as though the microphone was a telephone line to heaven. He lowered and raised his voice, pleaded with and praised the Lord, asked for forgiveness, and all in this smooth, patronizing voice that made me cringe. I wished more than ever that Renuka hadn't forced me to come, but when I looked across at her, I could see that she was fascinated, her head tilted down, but her eyes fixed on the glittering figure on the stage, who seemed to writhe with spiritual emotion.

After the prayer, he introduced the other members of his crusade, the band which travelled with him, each instrumentalist taking a bow and then plugging his guitar into an amplifier or taking his seat behind the drums or electric organ. All of them had a polished, glossy veneer, as though they had stepped right out of a television set and were not real but just a configuration of electric impulses. Their hair, their clothes seemed to emit a kind of luminous glow. Along with the band members there were eight young women who were called, 'The Holy Spirits'. Arthur Williams introduced them by their first names, Cheryl, Cindy, Megan . . . and they each had a gleaming smile. They wore blue mini skirts with a yellow buckskin fringe and they looked like cheerleaders at a football game. I had expected the worst but 'The Holy Spirits' left me completely overwhelmed by the obscenity of what was taking place.

Renuka was fascinated by the whole spectacle and even the boys were wide-eyed. The musicians struck up a tune and the 'Holy Spirits' sang a couple of gospel songs, swaying to the rhythm of the music. There was something very seductive about it all and if it weren't for the words of the songs, it might have been a musical review. Arthur Williams was like an Emcee and I could just imagine him playing the tape for his television audience back home and telling them about his wonderful experience with their 'missionary brethren' across the seas. Occasionally the cameras swung in our direction and the audience would get agitated, knowing that we were going to be on TV.

After the songs there were the testimonials which were even worse. One of the 'Holy Spirits', a platinum blond with a quavering voice, told us how she had been a sinful girl in high school and 'fooled around' with alcohol and drugs, and how the devil had led her into 'the worst kind of depravity, sex and the whole thing'. She had thought that she was having a good time but through it all she had been the unhappiest person in the world. To her, love was just something that took place on a Friday night in the back seat of a car. It was only when Jesus came into her life that she realized what 'true love' was all about. Love. She said the word over and over, as though by repeating it we would all understand what she meant. She said that one day, she had gone drinking with some friends and they had driven out to a party and it was going to be just like another night of sin, when suddenly she was touched by a deep and uncontrollable sadness and she knew that she would have to change her life. She asked her friends to let her out of the car right there on the highway. They thought she was crazy but she made them do it and after they drove off she began to walk back home. It was nearly ten miles but all the way she just kept thinking how terrible her life had become, when suddenly a yellow Corvette came by and stopped. Inside was a man who had the face of an angel and he asked her if he could give her a ride. At first she was frightened but something in his eyes made her trust him and she got into the car. As he drove her home, the man told her about Jesus and explained that he was the minister of a church in a nearby town. He talked and prayed with her and she began to cry and when they got home she asked him to come inside and he did and her parents woke up and they all sat around the kitchen table and they had some coffee and prayed together. After that she decided to dedicate her life to Jesus.

There was a predictable sameness to all of the testimonials. The blond girl wept as she told us how she was 'born again'. They sang another song and then one of the musicians told his story, how he had played for a rock group for several years and was really 'messed up' until he found the Lord. Arthur Williams told about their recent tour of Africa where he 'called forward' thousands of people to be saved, how in Nairobi they had filled a stadium full of 'native people' and they had all risen at once and praised the Lord. He told about a beggar in Cairo who had been saved by one of the Holy Spirits and a hippy in Greece where they had stopped for a day and a half. He had heard their message and accepted Jesus into his life. It was as though everywhere they went, people flocked to them and by the power of the Lord, they were 'saved'.

'Do you think it's true?' said Renuka whispering into my ear.
'I don't believe a word of it,' I said.
'But he's very persuasive,' she said. 'And I like his clothes.'
'I really don't find it funny,' I said.
Renuka grinned and patted my shoulder.

Arthur Williams launched into another song which every-body in the audience seemed to know except for us, and he encouraged the crowd to sing along until the gym reverberated with all those voices. It was like being inside one of the huge speakers on the stage. Looking around me, I could see peo-ple weeping, mothers holding their children's hands, others closing their eyes and singing out the song. I began to feel as though everybody in the audience had become possessed by some kind of supernatural force. I knew that Arthur Williams was manipulating them, building up their emotions to a cre-scendo through the music, through the testimonials, through his own frenetic energy. I would have walked out right then, except that we were seated in the middle of the bleachers and there was no way to escape without stepping over a dozen ec-static people, all moaning together in the chorus of the song.

When it ended there was a hush. Arthur Williams bowed his head over the microphone, as though listening for that one sound which would break the silence, but there wasn't even a whisper. Everyone had their eyes fixed on him. At last, he raised his head and began to speak in a quiet, almost sinister voice.

'Wasn't that a beautiful song, my friends? Sisters and Broth-ers. You have heard the music of the Lord. You have raised your voices in praise of the Lord. I ask you now to pray for those amongst us who have not seen the light, those who have turned away from the Lord, those who have yet to feel his love. Pray that they should come forward now, out of their darkness into the light. Let them stand up and show themselves to be God's children. Let them be born again . . .'

As he continued, pleading with the audience to step forward, the television cameras began slowly to pan across the bleachers, as if searching for those who needed redemption. I looked across at Renuka, almost expecting her to stand up. But she winked, as though to reassure me that she was still herself, unswayed by Arthur Williams and his crusade. Several others in the audience had already stood up and were moving forward, the people on the bleachers shifting aside to let them through. One of the guitarists in the band was playing lightly, in the background, as Arthur Williams' voice kept calling to the audience to come forward, like a deep, hypnotic chant. I felt as if I was in a nightmare, the crowded gymnasium, the bright lights and the throbbing music, wishing that I could escape the shame of what was going on. I felt as though I was the only one who could see what was really happening and I would never be able to stop it.

But just then, the electricity went off. One moment there was the brightness of the stage and the soft, pulsations of the guitar, the sound of Arthur Williams' voice; the next moment it was gone. The whole gym was in darkness, completely black. It was a usual occurrence on the hillside, but at that moment it came as such a surprise that for a few seconds nobody made a sound. After a minute, people started turning on their flashlights. A few of them shone the beams of light on Arthur Williams who stood helplessly on the stage, holding the dead microphone. His band and the 'Holy Spirits' peered back at the flashlight beams, uncertain what to do. There were whispers now and I could see the principal and Al Tyson running out the door. Tim had begun to flash his torch around but I made him stop. Renuka leaned over and asked me if I thought it was a sign from God.

'It's probably just a fuse,' I said. 'All that equipment must have been too much for the lines.'

We sat for a while, unsure of what was going to happen. Down on the stage, I could see Arthur Williams in a huddle with the other members of the group. Without his lights and microphone, he looked quite foolish, the sequins on his jumpsuit flickering in the flashlight beams. Everyone was getting restless and the high pitch of emotion had completely dissipated.

About fifteen minutes later, Mr Burley came up on the stage, very harassed. He raised his arms to make an announcement. Voices settled down and the flashlight beams converged on him, so that he had to shade his eyes as he spoke. He said that the lights were out all over the hillside and it seemed that one of the main switchboxes at the power station had burned out. They had telephoned the electricity department which said it would be at least an hour until the lights came back, and for that reason the evening would have to be adjourned. The audience groaned with disappointment. Mr Burley thanked Arthur Williams with a weak apology for the, 'unpredictable nature of our power supply', and asked us all to exit in a careful, orderly manner, through the doors at either end of the gym.

CHAPTER 7

TAFFY

Susan Carson

2 cups sugar
1 cup corn syrup
2 tablespoons butter

1/4 teaspoon peppermint flavour
green food colouring
1½ teaspoons salt

Grease the sides of a 2 quart saucepan. Mix sugar, corn syrup, salt and 1 cup water. Cook over medium flame, stirring constantly, until sugar is dissolved. Continue cooking without stirring until mixture comes to an even boil. Remove from heat; stir in butter. Add flavouring and colouring. Pour into a buttered pan. Cool until easily handled. Butter hands and pull taffy until it becomes stiff. Cut into fourths; pull into long strands and cut into bite-sized pieces. Wrap each piece in wax paper for storing.

'Wait a minute, Tim,' I said. 'What's this?'

'It's a recipe,' he said. 'For your cookbook. Susan asked me to give it to you.'

He was getting red in the face.

'Uh huh,' I said, eyeing him. 'Susan Carson.'

'It's really good. She made it yesterday when I was at her house.'

'I didn't know you were at her house,' I said. 'Yesterday, you said you were going down to the bazaar.'

'Well, I changed my mind,' he said, a little guilty.

'So you were making taffy all afternoon,' I said. 'That's nice. Susan's a nice girl.'

Tim nodded.

'I'm going steady with her,' he said, still not looking me in the eye.

'Going steady?' I said. 'Aren't you a little young for that?'

'Mom. I am in seventh grade. There are five couples in our class.'

'Well, it's not that I mind,' I said. 'I'm just a little bit surprised.'

Tim scowled at me. I looked down at the recipe.

'Maybe Susan could come over here some time and show me how to make this.'

That cheered him up.

'When?' he said.

'You'll have to check with her mother. What about Saturday?'

Tim thought for a moment, his face getting serious. I had the hardest time trying to keep from laughing.

'Okay, we'll need wax paper,' he said.

'I'll order some from the bazaar, and the rest of the ingredients,' I said.

'Can I go and tell her now?' said Tim.

'It's kind of late. Why don't you wait till school tomorrow? You'll see her soon enough.'

Tim frowned again and disappeared into his bedroom. I had to smile, even though it gave me a strange feeling thinking of him with a girlfriend. I could hardly believe that he was old enough but on the other hand kids these days seem more mature than we were at their age, or maybe I'm just forgetting what it was like. In any case, there wasn't much to worry about. Susan's mother, Mary Carson isn't the sort of woman to allow anything to get out of hand. I was actually surprised that she even let Tim into the house. She

88

and her husband are Pentecostal missionaries and very conservative.

Susan's a pretty girl, red-haired and freckle-faced, like something out of a Norman Rockwell painting. I always noticed her in Tim's class because she had a prim and proper way about her. At music concerts she would always do the solo parts and had a nice voice. Her whole family are musical and Mary Carson leads the community choir at church. She tried to get me to join one time but I told her that I was tone deaf and couldn't even hum a tune, which is the truth. I remember Susan played the lead role in the elementary school musical and she was wonderful, so full of life and singing with such confidence. It almost scared me, thinking of Tim going out with her. He's such a bumbler and she's so poised. Tim is going through an especially awkward, gangly stage and his voice is changing too, which makes him even more self-conscious.

After supper the boys got into a fight because Michael had been teasing Tim. I heard them shouting at each other and then Tim came out carrying his pillow and blankets which he'd torn off his bed. He was angry and on the point of tears, cursing and swearing under his breath. Going over to the sofa, he threw down his pillow.

'What's wrong?' I said, putting down the book that I'd been reading.

'I'm sleeping here tonight,' he said.

'What's Michael done this time?' I asked.

'He's been saying things,' said Tim.

'About you and Susan?' I said.

He nodded.

'Stay here for a moment,' I said. Leaving Tim sulking on the sofa, I went into their bedroom and found Michael sitting up in his bed grinning at me.

'Michael, why have you been teasing Tim?' I said.

'He's got a girlfriend. I saw them holding hands at recess.'

'There's nothing wrong with that.'

'It's Susan Carson,' he said.

'I know,' I said. 'And I don't think there's any reason for you to give him a hard time about it. Some day you're going to have a girlfriend and how would you like it if Tim teased you?'

'I'm never going to have a girlfriend,' he said.

'Don't speak too soon,' I said. 'Now listen to me. I don't want you to say anything more to Tim about Susan Carson. Is that understood? He doesn't need your opinions.'

'Okay,' said Michael, shrugging his shoulders. 'I only said that her hair was weird.'

'Lots of people have red hair,' I said.

'But her's is orange.'

'Now, hush,' I said. 'No more of this.'

When I went out into the living room again, Tim had already made himself comfortable on the sofa, pulling the blankets over his shoulders and pretending to be asleep.

'Tim. You can sleep in here if you like but I've talked with Michael. He won't tease you any more.'

'I'll kill anybody who says bad things about Susan,' he said.

'Come on,' I said. 'Michael just doesn't realize what it means to be in love.'

He didn't say anything more for a while and I picked up my book again, even though I wasn't really in a mood for reading. I had finished another page when Tim spoke up.

'Mom, when did you fall in love with Dad?' he asked.

I looked at him and shook my head.

'In college,' I said.

'Did you have any boyfriends before you met him?' he asked.

'A few,' I said.

'Did you ever have a boyfriend in seventh grade?'

'I really can't remember,' I said. 'That was a long time ago.'

'Have you ever told Dad about your boyfriends?' he asked.

90

'Some of them, yes,' I said.

'Did he get jealous?' asked Tim.

'No, I don't think so,' I said. 'Why do you ask?'

'Well, you see, before Susan started going out with me she was interested in Bobby Hermann,' said Tim. 'And now every time I think about him, I just want to beat him up.'

'That's silly,' I said. 'You're twelve years old. I don't mind you having a girlfriend but for goodness sake, don't take it that seriously. Couples go steady for a while and then they break up. It's not important at your age.'

'Well, I just think of Bobby holding hands with her and I want to murder him.'

'Timothy Manton, if this is the way you're going to be I won't let Susan come over to the house. Now the two of you should be having a good time together, not being jealous and spiteful about Bobby Hermann.'

'Susan says she doesn't care about him any more. She gave him back the ring he bought for her.'

'Well, there you are,' I said. 'That proves she's only interested in you.'

'Yeah, but it makes me worry about when we break up. I'll feel so terrible.'

'You really are the limit,' I said. 'You've just started going out with a girl and you're already worried about breaking up. That's no way to be. Now I don't want to hear another word. You get to sleep.'

When I told Renuka about Tim's girlfriend, she was delighted. She is always interested in what the boys are doing and wants to know everything about them.

'That's the wonderful thing about Americans,' said Renuka. 'They learn about love at such an early age. You let your children explore their emotions in a way that we would never allow in India. When I was a schoolgirl I would never have thought of having a boyfriend, especially not someone my parents knew about. If my father heard that I was seeing a boy, he would have beat me black and blue.'

'Well, this is fairly innocent,' I said.

'Of course, at their age it can't be anything else. It's so much healthier than our segregation. Your boys will grow up without being frightened of women.'

'It's strange, though, I really can't get used to the idea of Tim going steady. It's such a change for me.'

'Does it bother you?' said Renuka.

'I'm not worried about him, if that's what you mean, and I know there's nothing wrong with it. I guess it's just strange to think of him being interested in a girl.'

'Are you afraid of losing him?' said Renuka.

'Of course not. I have to accept the fact that he's growing up. I don't expect him to depend on me for the rest of his life.'

'And the fact that he told you about her all by himself means that he trusts you, doesn't it?' said Renuka.

'Sure. It isn't that. I don't feel possessive. I guess it's just that it makes me feel kind of old.'

Renuka laughed.

'You'll be a grandmother before you know it,' she said.

'Don't say that.' I said.

'What do you think they do together?' asked Renuka.

'Well, I know that the other day they spent the whole afternoon pulling taffy.'

'Pulling taffy?' said Renuka, 'That sounds perfectly obscene.'

'No, it isn't,' I said, impatiently. 'Taffy is a kind of candy and it's made by hand. You pull and stretch it until it gets a sticky consistency.'

'Do you think he's kissed her?' said Renuka.

'I doubt it,' I said. 'They're probably just holding hands.'

'You'll have to point her out to me some time. Is she very pretty?'

'She's cute enough,' I said. 'Red hair, very lady-like. She sings beautifully.'

'Maybe Tim will become musical,' she said.

'Heaven help us. He started clarinet lessons last year and that was terrible. You should have heard Tick howl, as though the world was going to end. Fortunately, he chipped a tooth and that put a stop to his musical career.'

'Poor Rachel,' said Renuka. 'It must be hard on you, seeing your son in love.'

'It's really not that bad,' I said.

'Do you think your husband will approve?' said Renuka.

'If he didn't he'd be a hypocrite,' I said.

'Was he very romantic when he was courting you?' she asked.

'In his own way,' I said. 'He's not a very passionate person.'

'Did you have a long courtship?'

'A year and a half. Frank was finishing up at medical school and we decided to wait until he had everything complete before we got married.'

'Did you sleep with him, before you got married?' said Renuka.

'Renuka! You're shameless,' I said.

'Just curious,' she said.

I looked at her and tried to keep from appearing too embarrassed.

'Yes, as a matter of fact, we did,' I said.

'I thought so,' said Renuka.

'Why do you say that?' I said.

'Because you're not the sort of person that goes entirely by the book.'

'Well, we were safely engaged,' I said. 'I didn't sleep with him until I knew for sure that we were getting married.'

'Doesn't that still qualify as adultery?' said Renuka.

'Technically, I suppose it does,' I said. 'But neither of us looked at it like that.'

'No, of course not,' said Renuka. 'You were in love.'

The way she said it, I could tell that she was teasing me. There was a mischievous look on her face, as though she found it very funny to think of me and Frank as lovers. Maybe she was just in one of her moods, or the news of Tim's first girlfriend had set her off, but I could tell that Renuka was laughing at me, not seriously, but just enough to make me feel exposed.

Susan did come over on Saturday and we made taffy together. It wasn't as awkward as I had thought it might be. She was not at all self-conscious, which was nice. Tim seemed a little embarrassed and hung around the kitchen door not knowing what to do, as we heated the syrup for the taffy. But once we had it made and he could help with pulling it, he seemed to relax. We talked about school and I asked Susan if she was going to be in any more musicals. She said that they were planning one next semester but her mother had told her that she could only take a minor part because she had so many other things to do. I was surprised how self-assured she was and it frightened me a little, the way she talked like a grown-up woman. Tim seemed so much younger than her, just a kid.

Michael had conveniently gone out with some of his friends for a hike to the limestone quarries, looking for fossils. He had known better than to stay at home while Susan was visiting. I think she gets on his nerves and I could see why, the way she behaves so properly. She pulled the taffy gingerly, as though it was beneath her dignity to get her fingers sticky. I had let her explain the recipe to me and the way she went over the instructions step by step, it was as though she were talking to a child. When I brought out a saucepan to make it in, she looked it over with a sceptical eye, as though it wasn't clean enough and made a comment about the stove not having a pilot light.

Anyway, Tim seemed to be completely under her spell and for his sake I didn't want to let myself get irritated with her. If Susan had been my daughter, I would have shaken her by the shoulders just to make her stop behaving like a prissy old schoolmarm.

After the taffy had cooled, Tim walked her home. I suggested that Susan take half of what we'd made but she said she was trying to 'cut down on sweets' and Tim could probably eat it all himself. She had a sugary way of talking about him that really made me clench my jaws.

It was quite some time before Tim returned, looking sheepish and going straight up to his room. I figured he wanted to be alone. Michael came back a little later, carrying a huge rock on his shoulder which he claimed was a dinosaur egg. I made him leave it outside in the garden, even though he wanted to put it on his shelf. He was covered with dust and full of stories about the fossils they had found. He wanted to know if he cracked the dinosaur egg in half whether he'd find a petrified baby inside. I said I doubted it and he had better have his bath before supper because I wasn't going to sit at the same table as an unwashed paleontologist.

Later that night, Tim came into my room. We hadn't spoken about the afternoon with Susan. He would never have talked about her with Michael listening.

'That taffy is pretty good, isn't it?' he said.

'Yes,' I said. 'It really sticks to your teeth.'

'Do you think you'll be able to use the recipe?' he said.

'I hope so. It will depend on how much space I have. We are planning to have a candy section.'

'Susan likes you,' he said.

'Well, that's nice of her,' I said.

'She said she didn't expect you to be the way you are.'

95

'What did she expect?' I said, cautiously.

'I don't know,' said Tim. 'She just said, she thought that you'd be different, more serious.'

'Well, you can assure Susan that I'm never serious,' I said.

'No, I don't think she meant it like that,' he said and I could see that he was struggling to remember exactly what Susan had told him. He tried again.

'She thought that you'd be older. She said she felt as though you were almost the same age as her.'

'Well, she's definitely wrong about that. You can tell her that I'm absolutely ancient.' Tim looked surprised and a little worried by my tone of voice. 'Now, go back into your room and tell Michael that he better have his homework finished when I come in, otherwise I'm going to roll his dinosaur egg over the side of the hill.'

About a week after Susan came over to make taffy at our house, I noticed that Tim seemed to have lost interest in her and was spending a lot more time at home. He didn't act upset or moody and I didn't really want to ask him what was going on. But I knew that he'd been planning to go over to Susan's house for a class party on the weekend and I asked him why he wasn't going.

'I've broken up with Susan,' he said.

'That's too bad,' I said.

'It's just as well,' he said, with a philosophical look on his face. 'We had a difference of opinion.'

'Is that so?' I said. 'What about?'

'Well, she's so conservative,' he said.

I nodded.

'Do you know what she told me?' said Tim. 'She said that Renuka was a sinful woman.'

'Did she really say that?' I said.

'Susan told me that she didn't approve of Renuka and that I shouldn't have anything to do with her.'

'Wait a minute,' I said. 'Is this what your argument was all about?'

'Yes, she said that Renuka is immoral because she drinks and has Hindu sacrifices at her house.'

'That's awful,' I said.

'I know. I told her that I didn't care if Renuka wasn't a Christian. I said it didn't matter and then Susan told me I wasn't a Christian either.'

'What a little shrew!' I said.

Tim looked at me, surprised.

'Well, I'm glad that you stood up to her Tim. I'm proud of you.'

'I don't like people who talk like that,' said Tim. 'If she'd been a boy, I would have hit her.'

I put an arm around him and kissed his forehead.

'Mom,' he said, 'you won't tell Renuka will you? I don't think we should.'

I shook my head. 'We'll keep it to ourselves,' I said.

I should have known that Jo Tyson and the other women weren't going to give up so easily. Even though I'd made my position very clear, that wasn't going to stop them from trying to convert Renuka. When Tim told me what Susan Carson had said to him, I got an uneasy feeling that there was going to be trouble. Susan had obviously got her opinions from her mother, who was a close friend of Jo Tyson. I thought about warning Renuka, but then decided there wasn't any point. She would just laugh and refuse to take it seriously. As it was, I never had a chance to intervene.

Renuka arrived at the house the evening after Tim and I had spoken. From the expression on her face, I could tell that something had happened.

'Rachel!' she said, 'I've just had the most bizarre experience.'

'What happened?' I said.

'This morning I got an invitation to have tea with Mrs Thompson. I've only met her once before but I thought I should accept to be polite. Actually, I assumed that you'd be there as well. When I got to her house, everything seemed quite normal. There were six or seven of them, Mrs Dupree, Mrs Carson and that Tyson woman. Those were the only ones I knew. We had some tea and biscuits . . .'

'Coconut cookies?' I asked.

'Yes. How did you know?' she said. 'Awful little gooey things.'

Renuka made a face, sticking out her tongue.

'I chatted with them politely and tried to behave myself as best I could because I got this feeling that they were all watching me. There was a kind of predatory look in their eyes. I kept wishing you were there because I felt quite out of place.

'As we were finishing tea, Mrs Thompson began this strange conversation with me about poetry and how she thought that all good poems should have a religious theme. I let her go on for a while, not really wanting to contradict her and also because I got the feeling that she was leading up to something else. After a bit she asked me if I was a Hindu. I told her that I was born a Hindu but I hadn't been to a temple since I was a child. This seemed to please her and then she said how glad she was that I had come to tea because she wanted to share something very important with me.

'I didn't know what was going on when they began arranging the chairs in a circle. When we were all seated again the women were watching me with earnest, bird-like faces. Mrs Thompson was on one side of me and taking my hand in hers, she went into this long explanation about Jesus Christ and how he died for my sins. She got quite emotional and in the middle of it all told me how her life was so much

98

fuller and more complete since she had accepted Jesus into her heart. The others nodded as she spoke and mumbled under their breath from time to time. What could I do but listen and brace myself for what was coming next?

'After she had finished, one of the women whom I didn't recognize took out a little cloth-bound Bible and read a few verses of scripture. Then they all joined hands and started to pray, going clockwise around the circle. Most of the prayers were about me and they kept pleading with God to open my heart to his love and all that sort of thing. They have such a pious way of talking. One of them even asked Jesus to tear the sin from my breast, which frightened me a little.

'During all of this I kept my head bowed, though I was watching out of the corner of my eye, their heads bobbing up and down as they moved their lips. It was a little like being at a seance except that we hadn't turned off the lights and nobody was calling up the dead. On the one hand I was absolutely fascinated, and on the other I was trying very hard to think of some way to escape. After they had each finished praying, I think they expected me to say something. Even though I was tempted to stand up and walk out, something kept me there, as if the force of all their prayers was holding me in my seat.

'I felt Mrs Thompson's hand on my shoulder and before I knew it, she was making me kneel down on the carpet. Then they all put their hands on my head and began to pray some more. This time though, the prayers sounded more desperate and they kept mentioning that I was sinful and God should save me from hell. I could feel their hands trembling. It was an odd sensation to have them all touching me, like being enclosed in a chrysallis. The whole thing was getting more and more absurd and I could feel myself starting to laugh. It was partly nervousness, I know, but there I was trying to hold back my giggles. You know how difficult it is to control yourself once you get started. Finally, I just burst out laughing.

Perhaps they thought I was shaking with religious fervour but pretty soon it became obvious that none of their prayers were working. Honestly, Rachel, I couldn't control myself. It was just so hilarious. In the end, I had to stand up. They were all taken aback and looked at me with alarm. There I was, still laughing like a hyena.

'Of course, as soon as I caught my breath, I tried to apologize but they just scowled and even Mrs Thompson looked angry. There was nothing I could do but get away as fast as possible. I said I was sorry for having been so uncooperative and thanked them for the tea.'

CHAPTER 8

BREAD AND BUTTER
PICKLE   **Astrid McKenzie**

2 cups cucumbers (sliced)   1 cup sugar
3/4 cup onions (sliced)   1/2 tsp. turmeric
1½ cup cauliflower florets   2 tsp. mustard seed
1/4 cup salt   1 tsp. celery seed
1½ cups vinegar   1/4 tsp. cloves (ground)
4 small sticks cinnamon

Mix cucumbers, onions and cauliflower with salt and 1/2 cup water.
Cover and let stand for 3 hours. Make a pickling syrup of the rest
of the ingredients. Bring to a boil for one minute. Drain cucumbers
etc. and add to the syrup. Heat over a low flame to scalding, using a
wooden spoon to stir. Pour into sterilized jars and seal or leave in a
large porcelain container.

I wasn't sure whether I should include my mother's pickle
recipe in the cookbook but it's one that I use all the time and
I've never tasted anything better. When we were children we
used to fight over the pieces of cauliflower, which would always
be eaten first, after which we would polish off the cucumbers.
My mother was the only one who liked the onions and my
brother Earl would drink the juice, pouring it into a glass — a
yellowish green colour. We would watch to see his face pucker
up and his eyes water after he drained the glass in one swallow.

My mother used to say it would make him sick but he seemed to like the taste and never let her throw the pickle juice away.

I haven't seen my mother for three years, not since our last furlough. She's the one who taught me how to cook and whenever I think of my mother, I picture her in the kitchen. We were a large family, made larger by a number of relatives who stayed with us in the old, white farmhouse which my grandfather built at the edge of a spruce forest outside the town of Hopkins, Minnesota. My mother was a good cook and she did everything on a shiny black, four-burner gas stove that used to stand in the corner of the kitchen. When I was very small, I remember an even older wood stove which stood against the opposite wall. My father and the other men used to go out to the copse beyond the hayfields and cut aspen branches during the summer and stack them in the woodhouse. My mother and my grandmother, who died the same year they took away the wood stove, used to bake bread and cakes and pies in the cast iron oven heated by the aspen branches, which were just the right size, about the diameter of my wrist when I was six years old. I remember the smoky smell that would sometimes seep out, and the way the big kettle used to boil on the stove top all day long. I remember my mother as a much younger woman than she is now, leaning over the kitchen table and kneading dough. I loved to watch the way her hands sank into the white mound of dough, the way she punched and pummeled it with her fists.

We didn't have central heating or indoor plumbing in the house until the year I went away to college. There was a wooden outhouse at the back and a sauna which my grandfather had built for himself near the pond. During the winter we always went into the sauna to get warm after ice-skating.

My mother never stopped cooking. That was her life and she would be the first one up in the morning while it was still dark. We would wake to the smell of sausage frying, cinnamon rolls and fresh coffee. Our house was quite a distance from the town and the school bus would reach our mailbox at seven each morning, so we had to be ready and waiting. During winter it would always be cold and dark when we got up but my mother would be there in her heavy flannel nightgown and one of my father's old woollen overcoats that she wore until the kitchen warmed up. My father would also be awake but we would seldom see him in the mornings, except sometimes when he would come in from the barn, blowing clouds of steam into the cupped palms of his hands, like a fire-breathing dragon. Sometimes there would be icicles on his moustache. Mother would give him a mug of coffee and hurry us along as we ate our eggs or pancakes. Before we knew it, the time would come for us to be out at the mailbox to meet the bus, that growling yellow monster that came rumbling down the dirt road. We would scramble inside and each of us would sit by a window and breathe on the glass so that we could write our names or rub out little circles through which we watched the dawn rising over the hayfields. Mother would always have our lunchboxes ready, peanut butter sandwiches for Earl because that was all he would eat and tuna fish or salami for the rest of us, and always a brownie or cookies which she had baked the day before. Her whole life was spent feeding us and the men on the farm who helped my father — they used to have appetites as big as the barn. She would cook for them all by herself. When I think about it I can't believe that she was able to do it on her own, along with all the other housework. Not only did she have to feed us and the farmhands but the animals as well, the two sheep dogs that we adopted one winter and the population of cats that lived beneath the porch and kept producing litter after litter each year. My mother would feed them too, with the same patience and love that she had for all of us.

When we would come home from school, she would still be there in the kitchen. It would be warm by now and full of the smells of baking. We would come inside and hang our bags and coats on the knobs which my father had screwed into the wall just at our height and my mother would have a snack ready for us at the table, milk and cookies or sometimes a piece of fresh pie. I began to help her in the kitchen when I was six or seven, though I was probably more of a nuisance at that age. Later my mother taught me with her own quiet, deliberate way of speaking, showed me how to knead the dough and how to make sausage and turkey stuffing and blackberry pies. My sister Alice was never very interested in cooking and the boys were only good for washing the dishes. They did that grudgingly and only because my father made them. Alice seldom showed any interest in the kitchen and she would get bored with cooking very quickly and go off to her room to read.

I was always happy working beside my mother in the kitchen. It was something I enjoyed as much as playing with Earl and Sam. She would tell me stories while we worked, stories about the sod house that she and her parents had lived in when they first came to Minnesota and the first winter they spent there, how the nearest neighbour was eight miles away, an hour by horse and carriage, except they didn't have a horse, and how the next spring my grandfather started to build the house even before the snow began to melt, cutting logs from the forest and dragging them on a sled. By that first summer he had three rooms built, the kitchen, the one bedroom which is where Earl and Sam used to sleep and a little store room where they kept their tools. Before the winter came he had also built his sauna, because that was the one thing he had longed for during the first winter in the sod house. By the end of autumn, when ice began to form on the pond, he had it ready. My mother told me how the whole family went down to try it out, all of them crowded into that one small space, sitting on the benches facing each other as my grandfather tended the fire and it got hotter and hotter until they were sweating and laughing so hard the sauna seemed as though it was going to break apart and then my uncle Swen suggested that they all run down and jump in the pond. As soon as he said it there was a race, the whole family, stark naked, running down to the pond and leaping through that first thin sheet of ice which had formed, so brittle that it seemed to break before they even touched it. I used to love my mother telling this story, the way she laughed. I could just see the whole family running naked out of the sauna and racing to see who would be the first one through the ice.

My father's family would never have done such a thing. They had come to America a generation before. They were Scottish presbyterians and very puritanical. My father was a hardworking man, sort of taciturn and strict with all of us. Mother used to whisper to me that my father was a little too prudish for her liking, though she loved him all the same. My mother didn't think there was anything wrong with her undressing in front of us, even when Earl and Sam were in high school. Sometimes, she and I would go down to the sauna just to sit and talk and be alone together. She used to say that it made her feel like bread dough, rising in a warm place. My father used the sauna only when he was older and had trouble with his arthritis, and even then he always wore his bathing suit.

There was something sad about my father. I think he felt as though he never really owned the farm because it had come to him from my mother's family. My grandfather had died several years before my parents got married and my uncle Swen had gone to college to become an engineer, so my father took over the farm as soon as he and mother got married. I don't think he had any ambitions beyond being a farmer but I think he resented working land which was never completely his own.

My father died two and a half years ago, soon after we returned from furlough. I was glad that we had seen him so recently and the boys got a chance to meet him, but I wished I could have been there for his funeral. He had been sick for several years with heart trouble, probably all my mother's pies and sausage clogging up ·his arteries. When we got the telegram about his death, I almost went back to the States, but it was a bad time for all of us. School was about to start and Frank was just getting back to work after the furlough. I was torn between wanting to be with my mother and having to get the boys settled into school. We had been there so recently it didn't seem to make much sense and I couldn't have made it back in time for the funeral, anyway.

My parents had been thinking of selling the old farmhouse for some time and after my father died, Earl wrote and said that he was trying to get my mother to move in with him, but she was stubborn and said that as long as she could look after herself she was going to keep the house. Her father had built the place and she intended to stay there until she dropped. Of course it was my father who had been the frail one and she was several years younger than him. Even today she's got plenty of energy and does all her own housework. There aren't so many people to feed nowadays, though Earl and his family come and stay with her from time to time and last year the daughter of one of my cousins, who wants to be a writer, spent a year at the farm working on a novel and keeping my mother company. We all worry about her but she seems so independent. Earl writes to me quite often and says that he thinks she is getting a little weaker. Her eyes have been a problem and I'm sure she misses my father even if he wasn't willing to run out naked into the ice.

We have a furlough coming up next year but sometimes I just feel like putting the boys in boarding and catching an airplane back home, just to spend some time with her while she's still able to stand near the stove and tell me those stories, just to be with her for a while, the two of us.

The other day Renuka asked me to show her some photographs of my family. I was surprised that she'd be interested, but once I got the albums out she wouldn't stop asking questions. It had been a long time since I'd gone through those pictures and I enjoyed showing them to Renuka and telling her about my parents and my brothers. She was especially taken by the pictures of the farm. It is a pretty place but she kept saying how it was just as she had imagined it would be, like something out of a Willa Cather novel. I think she has a romantic image of what a farm is like. I tried to tell her about the unpleasant things as well, like being snowed in for several days, and the time Earl almost lost his arm to the threshing machine, and those cold, March days, when the snow would begin to melt but spring would never seem to arrive.

Renuka wanted to know everything about my brothers, how many children they had, whether they still worked on the farm. But she was most interested in my sister Anne. In the pictures she is never in the centre, always off to one side with a kind of unhappy look about her. Anne and I were never very close. I guess it's like that sometimes, either you have a strong attachment to your brothers and sisters or you just get along with them as best you can. Anne is eight years older than me and my brother Earl is in between. I was the third and Morris was the fourth. My parents had us neatly ordered boy, girl, boy, girl. Anne was just that much older than me, so that I was always looking up to her and never quite mature enough to be her friend. She was already an adolescent when I was learning to walk. She was graduating from high school when I was just at the age when we might have been able to share our thoughts. But Anne's interests had grown beyond my understanding. We slept in the same room for several years but

Anne got impatient with me and she finally talked my father into fixing up the loft so that she could be alone. She's always been a solitary person and that's probably why it took her so long to get married.

'There is something about her in the pictures,' said Renuka, 'as if she were trying to hide from the camera.'

'I think she was just unhappy growing up on a farm. Anne wanted to be a city girl and as soon as she got a chance, she went away to New York,' I said. 'That was always her dream, to escape the farm and live in an apartment high above the streets.'

'She looks a little like you, but her eyes are very different,' said Renuka.

'I was a few inches taller than her,' I said, 'She resented that and I remember when she made my father buy her a pair of high-heeled shoes and we all made fun of her because the floorboards in our house were uneven and she kept twisting her ankle.'

'Poor thing,' said Renuka.

I was much closer to my brothers. They tolerated me and I was always able to play their games. Earl was just a year and a half older than me and Morris was two whole years behind, so I made it even for them. We would play baseball or cops and robbers. Anne was never interested and she would sit in her room up in the loft and shout down at us if we were making too much noise.

Now that I think about it, I probably resented the way she stayed aloof. I would have wanted her to be my friend, someone I could confide in. Earl and Morris weren't much good at that. I admired Anne from a distance, even though there wasn't much to admire in her. She was a mediocre student and not particularly popular at school. It wasn't as though I had to live up to her example. In fact my father always said that I was the most talented member of the family. He made me take piano lessons and do all the things that Anne refused to do. People always spoke of her as being "the quiet one". Of course, compared to Earl and Morris anyone was quiet. But Anne was different, she always seemed sort of reserved, not just with me but with everybody. I had boyfriends in school before she ever went on dates. It was a kind of awkward situation and I know my parents worried about her for a while.

Things turned out all right in the end. Six years ago she finally married an architect from Washington named Archer Botstein. I was so happy when I finally heard that Anne was getting married. I wrote her a long letter telling her things about myself that I had never shared with her before. I imagined that she would want to hear from me and I got carried away, telling her about Frank and the boys and the way we lived in India. It was the first long letter that I'd ever written to her. In some ways, I expected her to change, now that she was getting married, to come out of her shell and be my sister, listen to me in a way she'd never done before.

Anne wrote back a short, courteous letter, the same as she must have written to everybody else who sent congratulations, a quick thank you note and that was all. I was so disappointed. Frank had agreed to let me go home for the wedding and I had been all worked up, wanting to go back and see Anne walking down the aisle. But suddenly, when I got her letter, those four or five brief lines, without a trace of emotion and even the "Love," with which she signed her letter, so cold and meaningless, I just didn't want to go. I decided that I wouldn't attend her marriage. Why should we waste good money on my ticket home when she didn't seem to care?

Maybe I expected too much from her, but even Earl talks about her as though she were a stranger. The last time I visited him in Minnesota — he lives above twenty minutes away from my mother — Earl told me how he tried to keep in touch with Anne but she just seemed to get more distant with each year.

At one time he used to phone her every month just to see how she was doing but it got so frustrating after a while that he gave up. She and Archer live in Arlington, Virginia. He is a senior partner in a well known firm which specializes in making parking structures. They have a lot of money and haven't had any children and probably never will. Anne is forty-six and I just don't think she's interested in having a family. It would probably be a disaster anyway.

Frank and I visited them on our last furlough and we stayed in their home in Virginia, a huge split-level which Archer designed himself, very modern and nothing makes a sound. The doors close without a click, the toilets flush without a gurgle, the chairs don't creak when you move them. It's a beautiful home and Anne has filled it with all kinds of objects, Chinese vases and modern paintings, but it's absolutely lifeless. We stayed there for a weekend and the boys got so restless because they had to be on their best behaviour. The yard was one of those landscaped things where they couldn't play without knocking down the birdbath or trampling on the succulents. We were so glad to get away, I swore we'd never stay with Anne again. Archer is nice enough, but he seems to look down on us as though we're poor relatives from some backwoods place, further away than even Minnesota.

'Do you ever feel as though you want to leave India and just go back to your farm?' said Renuka.

'Sometimes,' I said. 'Of course, it wouldn't work that way. Frank isn't much of a farmer.'

'So, you just plan to live in India for the rest of your life?' said Renuka.

'I don't really know, Renuka. We've been here twelve years now,' I said. 'Frank talks about going back sometime but he's very happy in his work and at his age it would be difficult for him to start all over again.'

110

'But don't you ever feel as though you've cut yourselves off from your family, your childhood, your farm . . . or were you like your sister, always wanting to run away?'

'No. I never wanted to run away,' I said.

'But doesn't it seem unfair that you should be separated from your family?'

'I don't think I ever looked at it like that,' I said. 'It's not that simple, really. My family is pretty scattered. Morris moved to Florida a couple years ago and Anne's in Washington. Earl is the only one who's stayed near home.'

'Families are such peculiar things,' said Renuka, with a kind of wistful look. I couldn't help feeling a kind of troubled echo in her words and for just a moment she reminded me so much of Anne, the way she looked at me, as though I had something which she would never possess.

One day I admired a sari that Renuka was wearing. It was silk, a pale gold colour with intricate block printing along the border. The fabric had a crisp, smooth texture. The next day, she arrived at the house and gave it to me as a gift.

'But Renuka, you shouldn't be doing this,' I said.

'Why not? You said you liked it, didn't you?'

'Yes, but I've never worn a sari in my life,' I said. 'I don't even know how to put it on.'

'I'll show you then,' she said.

Renuka led me into the bedroom and told me to take off the dress which I was wearing. I tried to argue with her, but she was insistent and I finally had to give in. Standing there in my slip and bra, I watched as she unfolded the sari. Somehow I couldn't feel embarrassed with Renuka.

'I should have brought a blouse for you,' she said. 'You haven't got one I suppose.'

I shook my head.

111

'Then you can do without,' she said, 'The tribal women never wear a blouse.'

With that, she unfastened my bra and stripped it away from my shoulders with a casual sweep of her hand.

'What if someone comes around to see me?' I said, glad that I had locked the door.

'Don't worry, Rachel. They'll never recognize you in a sari,' said Renuka, drawing one end around my waist and tying a knot.

Then, very carefully, after wrapping the sari around again, she began to pleat it.

'I can't believe you've lived in India all these years and never worn a sari,' she said. 'It's the most wonderful garment in the world.'

'I always wanted to,' I said. 'But I guess I never had the courage to try. You know, I'd be so worried that it was going to come undone.'

Renuka laughed.

'That happened to me once,' she said. 'At a cocktail party at the British Council in Calcutta. There I was, chatting with this jolly English diplomat and suddenly I felt the whole thing coming loose.'

'What did you do?' I said.

'Well, I let it fall to the ground and tried to pretend that nothing had happened. The Englishman was far too drunk to notice. As soon as he gave me a chance, I grabbed the sari up and made a dash for the ladies room.'

All the time she was talking, Renuka was wrapping me in the yards of silk, adjusting the pleats, tucking them into my slip and making sure the length was right. I stood there helplessly, like a mannequin in a store window, feeling naked and exposed. There was something very pleasant about it too. I don't think anyone had ever dressed me, since I was a little girl.

112

'Isn't it odd, how a woman's breasts change after she's had a child,' said Renuka.

I couldn't help but laugh. She was draping the end of the sari across my shoulder and as she did, Renuka put her hand beneath one of my breasts and lifted it gently, as if she were examining a piece of fruit.

'Did you nurse the boys?' she said.

'Yes,' I said. 'Tim nursed until he was just over a year and Michael kept on much longer. I finally had to wean him when he was two and a half.'

'Did you enjoy it, feeding them?' she asked.

'Yes, I did. Except when they began getting teeth and started biting me,' I said.

Renuka stepped back and looked at me with a critical eye.

'There you are,' she said. 'Do you have a mirror?'

'Inside the cupboard door.'

I felt as though I was wrapped in a silk cocoon and when I saw myself in the mirror, it made me look so different, as if I had put on a disguise.

'Most western women don't look good in a sari,' said Renuka, 'but it suits you nicely. You have the perfect figure.'

I enjoyed her compliments, whether they were true or not. With Renuka I always felt much younger, not just another dowdy memsahib, but different in a way that is hard to explain, more alive, more aware of myself.

One night, I had a dream about Renuka. She and I were cooking an enormous meal, enough to feed the whole hillside. The kitchen was huge, full of pots and pans boiling over and strange medieval gadgets on the walls. There were just the two of us and I was trying very hard to follow the recipes in an old cookbook, from which the pages kept flying out. Renuka was adding things at random, spices and herbs, all kinds of unusual ingredients. She emptied a whole bottle of wine into one of the pots and when she tasted it, a delirious expression came over her face. I was frustrated and kept telling her to stop but it was as though she were intent on sabotaging the meal, confusing me completely, adding unexpected flavours to the dishes that I had prepared so carefully. The dream continued for a long time, until I finally woke up in a fit of temper and found myself alone in bed. It made me feel quite foolish, and when I told her about the dream Renuka laughed, throwing back her head and closing her eyes, as if she were trying to imagine what I had seen.

CHAPTER 9

A RECIPE FOR RACHEL

You were made to feed people,
Those hands of yours kneading the dough
For piecrust, for bread that rises at a different altitude,

(3 cups of wholewheat flour
1 pkt. dry yeast)

Here we sit in the mountains, high above
the ordinary ingredients. You are like a great she-animal
feeding her young from the countless nipples on your belly,
belly-up to those mouths, the nestlings. Your whole life is
feeding, feeding two strong boys, who are approaching
their first experience of love, having loved you all this time,
now ready for girls who remind them of their hunger.

(2 tablespoons sesame seed oil
1 egg yolk)

Am I embarrassing you, Rachel?
Am I saying the kind of thing that makes you blush so beautifully?
My chef . . . make me a layer cake with orange frosting or
a
cold
cucumber soup. Start with the strong ingredients and make it
a tasteful poem, not like my insipid recipes.

(vinegar and garlic, ginger and fenugreek,
add cardamom and the pungent oil of cloves to kill
pain and sadness)

The invisible shadow of the mountains
Makes me want to hold you

And feed upon the fruit of your tree

(apricot and plum)

Let the boys climb to the top of the ridge
While you and I remain
In the valley of my poems.

Renuka gave me the poem just as she was leaving the house. I
could tell she wanted me to wait until she'd gone before I read
it, the way she handed the sheet of paper to me and moved
toward the door. I glanced at it.

'For me?' I said.

'Yes, it's something I wrote this morning when I got up. I
hope you like it.'

I wanted to thank her but she had already turned and gone.

Taking the poem inside, I sat down on the sofa in the living
room. Renuka had written the poem on a piece of lined paper
with two holes punched in the side, like the paper the boys use
at school. She had obviously copied it out carefully because her
handwriting was much neater than when she wrote me notes or
messages. It took me a moment before I could read the poem.
I just stared at the pattern which the words made on the page,
as though it were a picture she had drawn and not a poem.

I found that for some reason I could not read it silently.
My eyes kept skipping forward and then back again, as though
I was impatient to reach the end. Finally I read it aloud to
myself, one word at a time, until the meaning of the lines
came through and I could understand what she had written.
Sometimes there seemed to be more than one meaning to her
words, the way she broke apart the phrases and stanzas, as if
she meant for me to crack the poem open like an egg. It was so
personal that I found my hands trembling, not so much because

116

it moved me — it was not that kind of poem. There were some she wrote that made me cry. This one was different. It was as though I could hear her voice reading it to me and she was saying things which were meant only for me to hear. I kept going over each line again and again to try and understand exactly what she meant. Maybe I wasn't supposed to read it in that way but instead, just to let the words affect me however they might.

Poetry has always seemed to be such a mysterious thing. When I was in college I used to write poems but they were always silly, sentimental rhymes. I would have been too embarrassed to show them to anybody or even to admit that I had tried writing them. I couldn't judge if Renuka's poems were good or not but there was something in them which affected me. I liked the way she described things and I was surprised how easily she seemed to capture a feeling or an image.

Maybe if I didn't know her . . . maybe if I had just read her poems in a magazine, I wouldn't have thought very much about them, but because they were Renuka's I felt attached to what she said. I did feel a little embarrassed about some things, like the line about the 'countless nipples on your belly,' and I don't think I could ever show the poem to Tim or Michael. I thought of sending a copy to Frank and wondered what he'd think. Probably he wouldn't even read it all the way through, or he might just assume it was some kind of joke. He doesn't like poetry very much. Even if he did, I don't think I would send this poem to him. It's something between me and Renuka and no one else, a secret which I am meant to keep.

Because most of her poems were written in Bengali, I was able to read only those which she had translated. Sometimes Renuka would read out loud to me in Bengali or recite a poem or two. I enjoyed hearing just the sound of the language, the cadence of the words, her voice becoming lower and more expressive. As she read to me, Renuka would explain each line,

117

though often I could see her frustration because there was no perfect English equivalent.

Renuka could go on for hours about the Bengali language, telling me how it was full of the most evocative images, more lyrical than French or English. As for Hindi, she called it a bureaucratic language, contrived and lifeless. English she would say, 'is such a basic language. You can only say so much with it. There are only a handful of ways to describe passion whereas in Bengali each word is ripe with passion. In English you have to pile on the adjectives until it becomes overloaded and you still can't catch the essence of a thought. French is better. I studied it for several years and there is nothing like one of Rimbaud's poems to give you the excitement of words. But even French is a drab language when you compare it to Bengali. You should read Moliere's plays translated into Bengali. They take on a whole new dimension. The thing about Bengali is that it's an alluvial language; all the fertility of Sanskrit and the other northern languages have washed into Bengali. Each word is a poem.'

'I think everybody feels that way about their mother tongue,' I said.

'No. No. I'll prove it to you,' she said.

Renuka opened one of the drawers in her dressing table and took out a small copy book. It looked more like something in which you'd keep accounts. On each page, I could see that she had written lines and stanzas of poetry. The lettering looked quite ornate with curls and twists to it, much more attractive than Hindi lettering.

'These are poems that I'll never be able to publish,' said Renuka, leafing through the copy book.

'Why not?' I said.

'Because they're my erotic poems,' she said with a mischievous expression. 'I think every poet writes erotica of one kind or another but it usually gets discovered only once they die.'

118

Taking a deep breath and holding the book in both her hands she began to read. At first, the poems sounded no different from others I had heard. Of course, I couldn't understand a word, but gradually her voice began to change. She hardly looked at the pages and it was almost as though she were speaking to me instead of reading. Her eyes would wander around the room and then suddenly she would stare at me with such intensity that I had to look away. Renuka might have been reading any kind of poem for all I understood, but as I listened I could hear an unmistakable undertone of sensuality in the words. Maybe it was the way she looked at me, her eyes so large and full of emotion.

It could have been my imagination but as she went from poem to poem there was no mistaking the physical tension in the words, something deeply sexual.

I realized that Renuka was teasing me with the poems and maybe exaggerating the sensuality in her voice. I wished I knew the meaning of the words. Just the rhythm and tempo of the verses seemed to express the passions of two people making love. On one hand I found it so disturbing that I wanted her to stop but on the other hand I was fascinated by the way the poems affected both of us. I sat absolutely still, my hands pressed between my knees. Renuka was leaning forward, almost crouching in her chair and I could hear her breath catching at the end of each phrase.

After maybe half an hour — it could have been longer, I couldn't tell — Renuka finally put down the book and covered her face.

'Sorry, Rachel,' she said. 'You must be very bored.'

'No,' I said. 'Don't stop.'

Renuka peered up at me with an anxious look. I could see that there were tears in her eyes though she had got control of herself.

'I'm making a fool of myself,' she said.

'You aren't,' I said. 'When did you write those?'

'Some of them I wrote a long time ago. There are a few recent ones. I've never read them to anyone before.'

She had rolled the copy book into a tube, as if to seal it up like an ancient scroll. I didn't ask her to explain the poems and she offered no translation. It was as though I didn't need to ask the meaning.

I knew that Renuka got depressed sometimes and her moods would change in minutes, but she was careful not to let me see her melancholy side too often. Even though she seemed so strong and independent, there were days when I could tell that she was upset, the way she looked at me, her eyes searching for something, as if there had been a flower in her hand, or a bright coloured feather and it had suddenly disappeared. She would get a disturbed expression on her face, a look of disappointment. Even then, I think she was happy living by herself and writing poems. When I read what she had written about the 'invisible shadow of the mountains', I thought how much it was like her own sadness which she made invisible, those shadows which I could never see but I knew were there. She told me once that she wrote best during the night, when she would wake up, unable to sleep. Renuka would then sit and write, sometimes until dawn, the words streaming from her pen. This was how I imagined her, though I never actually saw Renuka writing and whenever I visited her she would be doing something else, sitting in the garden, reading a book.

I think I would go crazy with nothing to do, but Renuka seemed to thrive on it. Her servant, Savitri did all of the house work, even made her bed. Renuka did a little gardening from time to time but most of the flowers at Erinfell were perennials and came up on their own. Being by herself, there was nobody else for her to look after, no responsibilities. I sometimes envied her the way she seemed to have so much time on her hands. I would often arrive at Erinfell and find her still in bed at eleven o'clock in the morning. Her baths would take forever. She was never in a hurry and our meals together would stretch on for hours as she picked at her food. It wasn't that she was indolent or lazy. When something caught her interest she would spend long hours working on it, like the sweater that she decided to knit for herself last spring. Renuka had never knitted in her life before but she chose a complicated pattern from a magazine and spent forever working out each of the stitches, sometimes taking an hour to finish a single row. She became absorbed in knitting.

'It's the first time I feel as though I'm doing something practical,' she said. 'My poems are nothing but words. You can't touch them. You can't eat them. You can't wear them. But this sweater. I feel as though I'm really making something useful.'

In the end, Renuka's sweater never got completed. She had finished the difficult part, the front panel with its intricate design and one sleeve, but that's as much as she got done. When I didn't see her working on it for several days, I asked her about the sweater and she said that she was planning to finish it later on but for the moment she was working on a short story and after that was done she might go back to knitting. Besides, it was summer now and she had a long time yet before she would need to wear a sweater.

One of the things that always fascinated me about Renuka was her relationship with Savitri. Both of them were unusual women. Savitri looked as though she'd just stepped out of a village. Her clothes were those of a traditional hill woman, a black skirt with embroidery along the hem. With this she wore a tight blouse which fastened across her breasts and around her head she would wrap a bright yellow shawl which made her look as though she was carrying a bundle on her head. The only time she would unwrap the shawl was when she was working in the kitchen or doing the sweeping. Even though

Savitri was Renuka's servant there was a closer relationship between the two of them, a kind of affectionate bond. Often when I visited Renuka, Savitri would come into the room and squat down between our chairs and join in the conversation. Occasionally Renuka would shoo her out, but many times she would make Savitri tell us things about her village and her family. Usually these were things which she had confided in Renuka and which would then be repeated for my benefit. I always found it amusing because Renuka and Savitri came from such separate worlds, even more different in some ways than Renuka's and mine.

Savitri's village lay several ranges back in the mountains. She had been married when she was thirteen or fourteen to a man nearly twenty years older than herself. As it happened, they had no children even after five years of marriage. Savitri tried everything to get a child, prayed at temples and shrines which promised fertility, kept all her fasts, ate herbal remedies that made her sick for weeks, but still she could not get pregnant. Finally her husband gave up on her and took another wife who bore him a son within the first year. Even though she was much younger than Savitri, the second wife became the favourite in the house and Savitri was treated like a servant. For a number of years she lived with this humiliation and continued to try and find a cure. Each year the second wife would produce another child and Savitri would feel even more miserable than before. Mendicants and medicine men who passed through her village offered all kinds of advice and remedies. They told her to bathe in Ganges water mixed with milk or to eat nothing that was grown beneath the ground. Still desperately hoping to have a child, Savitri offered them whatever jewelry and coins she had.

Finally, one of her brothers-in-law approached her. Several times before he had tried to seduce Savitri but she had refused to sleep with him. He was even older than her husband and crippled in one arm. Her brother-in-law laughed at her and told Savitri that she was a fool to turn him down. He said that she was sure to get pregnant by him if only she gave him the chance. In a sly, confiding tone, he told her that all of the children whom the second wife had borne were actually his. He also told her that his brother knew about the arrangement. All this time Savitri had been convinced that she was barren and now she learned it was her husband's fault. He had let his brother sleep with the second wife just to protect his pride.

I heard Savitri tell her story one night at Renuka's and as I listened, I was amazed by the frankness of her voice and that after all those years of suffering she could still laugh at herself. Discovering what her husband had done, she decided to leave him and came away from her village looking for work. A cousin of hers was married to one of the cooks at the school and having nowhere else to go she arrived on the hillside around the same time that Renuka had rented Erinfell. Even though Savitri had never worked for anyone before, Renuka hired her and she had been at Erinfell ever since.

At one point Savitri's husband, finding out where she was living, had come to fetch her back but Renuka told me how Savitri had chased him away, calling him every imaginable name, from an impotent corpse to a son of a pig.

Both Renuka and Savitri each had a terrible temper and sometimes they would fight between themselves. At least twice, Savitri had packed up and left the house, swearing that she would never come back, but there would always be a reconciliation and soon enough I would find them together again.

Savitri often complained to me about Renuka and told me how unfair she had been, or the irrational demands she made, but at the same time Renuka would tell me how impossible it was to have Savitri around the house because she was straight out of the village. They would squabble all the time. One day Savitri used Renuka's shampoo to wash the clothes. Another day she left the iron on and burnt a hole in one of Renuka's saris. There was a constant give and take to their relationship which I don't think I could have lived with. Bindru has his problems but essentially he and I have worked things out so that we have very little to do with each other. With Renuka and Savitri, I got the feeling that they actually enjoyed harassing each other. It was like a game. Sometimes one of them would be angry and sulking and other times they were like the closest friends, laughing and teasing each other, playing practical jokes, calling each other names.

The two of them made quite a pair and in a strange way I got the feeling that they suited each other. Even though I was her closest friend on the hillside, I don't think Renuka felt as comfortable with me as she was with Savitri. I knew that during those long winters at Erinfell when I was away in Ranchi and the hillside was deserted, the two of them sat together for hours in front of the fire place and told each other stories. At times like that they were not servant and mistress but more like a pair of sisters who had shut themselves away from the world and shared their loneliness in the seclusion of the mountains.

'I tried to commit suicide once,' said Renuka, 'but of course, I botched it up.'

'How could you?' I said.

'Well, I'm very good at botching things up,' she said.

'No, I mean how could you have even considered suicide?' I said.

'I knew you'd get upset if I told you, Rachel,' said Renuka, 'but it happened such a long time ago and I don't think I could ever bring myself to try it again.'

'I should hope not,' I said.

'It was at a time when I was very unhappy. I was sick of living in Calcutta. My friends all seemed so shallow and self-absorbed. My family, as usual, were being difficult. I was desperate for something different, another life perhaps.'

'What did you do?'

'I wasn't very imaginative. I took a bottle full of tranquilizers but then, as soon as I had swallowed the pills, I decided to call a doctor friend and offer my organs to anyone who needed them. I wanted to do something useful with my body, share it around, donate my kidneys here, my heart over there, my cornea in someone else's eye. Of course, the doctor arrived at the house in plenty of time to save me and when I woke up I was very disappointed because I'd expected to be divided out amongst all these other people and here I was, still in one piece.'

'Stop it, Renuka,' I said. 'You're making it up.'

'I'm not. Honestly,' she said.

Renuka had a way of turning everything into a joke, but I knew that she could become very depressed. One day I dropped in to see her unexpectedly. After knocking for some time I heard her voice from inside the house but nobody came to answer the door. Going in, I found Renuka lying on her bed, dishevelled, her hair uncombed, wearing only a bathrobe. Her face was drawn and haggard and she looked at me as if we'd never met before.

'Renuka, are you okay?' I said.

She didn't move and spoke in a muffled voice.

'Go away, Rachel,' she said.

'What's happened to you?' I said.

'It's only a migraine,' she said, softly. 'Let me be for a while. I'll be all right. Don't worry.'

'Have you taken any medicine?'

'No,' she said. 'It will go away on its own.'

'Can I get you anything?'

'Nothing, Rachel. I think it would be best if you just left me alone. I'll get better soon.'

She lay there with her face turned towards the wall.

'Are you sure you don't want me to stay?' I said.

She said nothing but lay there like a sulking child. I sat beside her on the bed for a while. I knew it wasn't a migraine. Wanting to comfort her, I put my hand on Renuka's shoulder but as soon as I touched her, she pushed me away.

'Leave me alone,' she said, her voice sharp and angry.

I was so startled that I stood up. I felt as though I should try to help her but at the same time I was uncertain about what to do and I was also a little frightened to see her like this. Leaving the house I felt helpless, knowing that something was wrong but Renuka would never tell me what it was.

Savitri was sitting in the sun outside Erinfell. She always greets me with a smile but today she also seemed to be depressed.

'What has happened to the memsahib?' I asked her.

'I don't know. This morning she yelled at me for no reason and threw a book at me. I am tired of working for a witch like her. I am going to quit.'

'Don't say that. She is sick,' I said. 'I'm sure she didn't mean to yell at you.'

'No, memsahib, she is not sick. She is crazy.'

I knew there wasn't much point in talking with Savitri and hated to leave Renuka like this, but there was nothing to do except go home. All the way back to Murchison, I felt miserable for Renuka. I liked to think of her as a friend but at a time like this she pushed me away. I wanted so badly to help her, to hear whatever might be troubling her, but it was as though she wanted to be left alone in her misery. I felt angry and frustrated with her for not letting me stay and comfort her.

When I got home, I tried to ignore the uneasy feeling which kept coming over me, but I couldn't get Renuka out of my mind, the sight of her lying there in that shabby dressing

126

gown, the room all upside down, a sour smell of alcohol, the curtains drawn. I knew that there was something wrong but I didn't know what it could be.

The next day she arrived at Murchison with a huge bouquet of wildflowers, full of apologies for what had happened.

'I'm sorry for being such a bitch, Rachel,' she said. 'I didn't mean to be so rude yesterday. I was just feeling awful.'

'It wasn't a migraine was it?' I said.

Renuka smiled.

'Of course it was. I get them all the time. Sometimes it's worse; I feel as though my head is going to break into a thousand fragments.'

'I think you were upset about something.'

Instead of answering, Renuka began to help me arrange the flowers in a vase.

'I wish you'd tell me the truth sometimes,' I said. 'If we're supposed to be such close friends, then why can't we share our unhappiness as well as the good times, Renuka?'

She took one of the wild larkspurs from the vase and snapped the stem with her finger nails. Then playfully she reached across and put it in my hair.

'I've hurt you,' she said.

'Yes, you have,' I said. 'I just feel as though you're hiding part of yourself from me.'

Renuka took another flower, this time a sprig of wild ginger, and threaded it into the button hole of my blouse. She had a playful expression on her face. Her hand reached up and touched my cheek.

'You're right, it wasn't a migraine. I was depressed, that's all.'

'Depressed about what?' I said.

She turned away.

127

'I don't know,' she said. 'Just everything. But it's over now. Let's not talk about it. Let's forget those sort of things. Let's go for a walk.'

'I can't,' I said, 'I have the dhobi coming in half an hour.'

Renuka laughed.

'You're angry with me,' said Renuka.

'No, I'm not angry,' I said, 'I just want you to be honest with me.'

'What do you want me to tell you?' she said. 'Do you want me to tell you that I hate to live alone, that I'm miserable by myself, that I wish I was married and that I had a husband and two handsome sons like you? Do you want me to tell you that I wish I could cook and sew like a real woman? Do you want me to say that I'm unhappy with my life and I sometimes get so depressed that I become suicidal? Is that what you mean by being honest, Rachel?'

She spoke in a flat monotone which was so different from her usual voice.

'Is that the way you feel?' I asked.

'No,' said Renuka. 'It's not that simple. If it was, I would have killed myself a long time ago.'

Renuka and I would go for walks at least twice a week. We would set off in no particular direction, along one of the many trails that criss-crossed the hillside. It was nice to be outdoors and Renuka would collect things on our walks, a snail shell or a feather, a piece of lichen or a coloured stone which caught her eye. I never picked things up because I liked to have my hands free but she seemed to need something to hold, something which she could take back home with her.

One of our favourite places to go for walks was Burnt Hill, a small ridge to the east of the hillside. It was about a mile and a half from Murchison and we would often take a picnic with us when we went. The place was called Burnt Hill, because forest fires had destroyed all of the trees on the southern slope and left it bare. A footpath circled the hill and led down to a nearby village. From a distance, Burnt Hill didn't look like a very attractive place, but from the top there was a beautiful view of the snow mountains and there was a thick forest on the northern slope.

At the top of Burnt Hill there was a single grave, which we discovered on one of our first visits there. It was covered with a simple slab of granite which was discoloured by lichens and moss, the inscription almost erased with time.

SACRED
To The Memory of
A Devoted Wife And
Matchless Friend
MARGARET
The Wife Of
Captain A. G. Proctor
HM 10th Foot
January 29th, 1851

It was a simple, touching inscription. I asked Mrs DeSouza, who usually knows everything about the town, but she had never heard of Margaret Proctor. There was no mention of how she died or whether she had any children or even how old she was, but the fact that she was not buried in the graveyard near Hoburn church seemed unusual.

Renuka and I had an ongoing argument about the grave. She was convinced that Margaret Proctor had done something scandalous and terrible, something which had made her an outcaste on the hillside. For that reason she had not been buried in the cemetery. I disagreed with her. My theory was that the hill had been a favourite place of hers, just as it was for us, and when she died her last wish had been to be buried there on the top of the hill, facing the snows.

129

'Why do you have to be so romantic?' said Renuka. 'Can't you see, those British bastards buried her here, as far away as they could. I'm sure she must have had an affair or something.'

'But what about the inscription?' I said. 'Her husband wouldn't have called her a "matchless friend and devoted wife" if she'd done something like that.'

'Maybe he loved her despite what she had done.' said Renuka, 'I still think there's a mystery here which we will never uncover.'

One day when Savitri heard that we were going to Burnt Hill she told Renuka not to go. She claimed that the hill was haunted and that was why it had burned. According to Savitri, Margaret Proctor's ghost attacked one of the milkmen from the village on the north side of the hill. She broke his arm and left a mark on his forehead. The man had gone looking for one of his cows which had strayed and he could remember nothing of what happened except that he found himself lying near the grave with a broken arm and a painful bruise in the middle of his forehead. Savitri told us that most villagers stayed away from the hill, especially after dark, and each year the milkman would go and light an oil lamp at the grave to placate the spirit of Margaret Proctor.

CHAPTER 10

ALMOND CHICKEN   **Muriel Sing**

1½ lb. chicken breast sliced thin	1/2 Tbs. salt
1 cup almonds, shredded	3 Tbs. oil for frying
1/2 cup cooked ham, shredded	2 scallions or 1/2 onion diced
1½ Tbs. soy sauce	1 thin slice ginger
2 Tbs. vinegar	
1 Tsp. sugar	

Heat skillet (350 F). Add oil, heat thoroughly. Quick fry scallions and ginger for one minute. Add chicken and ham. Stir for 4 minutes until almost done. Add sauce and quick fry for 2 minutes. Add almonds, stir for 1 minute. Serves four.

Muriel Sing is the wife of the Chinese shoemaker and she has been a member of the Women's Club for years, a quiet little woman with her hair pulled tightly back in a bun. She and her husband are Christians and they came across from China after the revolution. They had been close to many American missionaries in Shanghai and always attend church each Sunday. Muriel is rather shy and hardly ever goes out without her husband. Her English isn't very good and I never know what to say to her.

I don't go down to the bazaar very often, since I can buy almost everything we need from the 'wallahs' who come door to door. The chowkidar goes to the bank and the post office every day and does whatever shopping needs to be done. The town is very different from the hillside and I've never liked it all that much, especially during the tourist season, when crowds of young men on holiday pass remarks and act smart. The boys go down on Saturdays to see the English movie at the Odeon. They like to eat downtown in one of the sweetshops and go to the shooting galleries along the mall. Practically the only reason I go down to the bazaar is for my shoes. Mr Sing is the only person who can make a shoe that fits my foot. My arches are especially high and most shoes are either too loose or too tight. Mr Sing has somehow figured out my feet and I always get my shoes from him, even though they cost a little more. The boys tease me about my shoes and so does Frank. He can't understand why I don't buy them off the shelf at Bata and be done with it. He says it's an extravagance; well, it's the only one, I say and he can put up with it as far as I'm concerned.

The boys hate it when I go downtown with them because it means they can't run loose as usual. I don't do it very often, so I expect them to show a little patience with their mother once in a while.

I ordered a pair of suede pumps last week and Mr Sing had asked me to come in for a fitting on Saturday, so I took the boys along, promising them a Tutti Frutti if they didn't complain too much. Mr Sing has a small glass-fronted shop near the roller skating rink. There is a simple signboard above his door.

Lee Tung Sing
Chinese Bootmakers and Accessories

It's one of those quaint old places that never change, always smelling of leather and crepe rubber, a sweet smell. One time I came to the shop and Mr Sing offered me a cup of jasmine tea. He's always very polite. He must be over seventy but his face doesn't show it, the colour of pale kid leather, smooth and unblemished. He seems to have very few customers and never hurries over his work.

While we were waiting for Mr Sing to get the shoes from his work room, the boys were fidgeting, glancing around the glass cases lined with men's dress shoes that are always on display and never seem to sell or change. I don't know how Mr Sing stays in business since nobody except for me seems to buy his shoes. His father was the one who started the shop. The whole family came over from China together and lived in Calcutta for many years. Mr Sing told me all about it one day and how he'd gone to a mission school in Shanghai for a couple of years until they sailed out to Calcutta. He said he always had a good relationship with missionaries.

'Hey, look at these,' said Tim.

He was pointing to a pair of riding boots with laces all the way up from the toe, almost thirty or forty eye holes.

'Weird,' said Michael.

Mr Sing came back with my shoes, the tongue and sole not cut completely and the stitching roughly sewn together. As he was helping me fit it on with the shoe horn, holding my foot by the ankle, he said.

'Good boys you got, Mrs Manton.'

'Thank you,' I said, catching Michael's eye with a meaningful look.

'What about some shoes for them?' he said.

'All they ever wear are sneakers,' I said.

Tim and Michael had that impatient, churlish look that they get when they know I'm talking about them.

'I could make them each a pair of hiking boots,' said Mr Sing.

'What do you think, Tim? Would you like a pair of boots?' I asked.

'Like these?' he said, pointing to the riding boots.

Michael laughed out loud and I thought Mr Sing would get offended.

'How's the fit?' he asked, as I stood up and felt my shoes, moving my toes and taking a few steps back and forth.

'Yes, they're fine Mr Sing. You always get them right,' I said.

'It's the lasts, Mrs Manton. I have one special just for you,' he said, taking off the shoe.

'Hey boys,' he said, 'You ever seen a leopard?'

Tim and Michael looked blank. They shook their heads.

'Come here,' said Mr Sing, holding back the curtain which hung across the doorway to his workroom. 'Show you something.'

They followed him into the workroom as I put on my old shoes again. A minute later, I heard Michael say something in a low voice. I pulled the curtain aside and looked to see what it was. The workroom was lit with a tubelight and it was poorly ventilated. Instead of the pleasant odour of sweet leather there was the stink of glue. On one wall, facing the door, was a leopard skin, with the head mounted and resting on a chest of drawers. It was tacked up on the wall with its legs and tail outstretched. The head was set in a scowling grimace, the mouth drawn back to show the teeth. Tim and Michael were staring at the leopard in amazement.

'Man-eater,' said Mr Sing.

'Wow, really?' said Michael.

'It killed thirty-two people in three years,' said Mr Sing. 'Look at the teeth. All broken. An Englishman, he shot it.'

'Where's the bullet hole?' said Tim.

'Back here,' said Mr Sing, pointing above the shoulder.

'Where'd you get it from?' said Michael.

'My father, he was a taxidermist,' said Mr Sing. 'He just make boots for money. But really he was an expert at this. Lot of Maharajahs used to get him to do their tiger skins. He make them look alive. The Maharajahs, they would joke because we got the same last name, Sing, like them. He stuffed all kinds of animals for British hunters too. This one, he did a special job because it is a man-eater. But the Britisher he ran out of money and couldn't pay my father. He told him to keep the skin and give him a pair of shoes instead. My father did a real good job. The coat still smooth and he look just like he's ready to eat another hundred people.'

Tim had finally got up the courage to touch the leopard skin and he ran his fingers over the glossy fur, with its pattern of black rosettes. Michael put his hand in the mouth and felt the broken canines. I thought, maybe now they'll get Mr Sing to make them each a pair of Sunday shoes. That's what they need more than hiking boots.

'Neat, Mom, isn't it,' said Michael, looking round.

'Look at those claws,' said Tim.

Mr Sing smiled at the two of them.

'A lot of people offer me to buy this leopard but I never want to sell,' he said.

'Do you know how to stuff a leopard, Mr Sing?' said Tim.

'Oh yes, my father taught me,' he said. 'But now I don't do these things. Takes a lot of practice.'

'Come on, what about that Tutti Frutti?' I said.

Tim and Michael turned away reluctantly.

'Send your chowkidar on Tuesday, Mrs Manton. Please. Your shoes be ready then.'

'Thank you, Mr Sing,' I said, waving as we went outside.

The Carlton Hotel is one of the oldest buildings in the bazaar. It was built back in the twenties and used to be a popular dancing place, according to Mrs DeSouza. The hotel stands above the mall with a restaurant on the first floor. The whole place is a little run down and there are several modern hotels which charge much less and offer more comfortable rooms. The restaurant is still popular, though, and it has a

135

nice atmosphere, a quiet refuge from the bustle and noise of the bazaar.

The boys and I got a table next to the windows overlooking the mall. It's always fun to watch the tourists promenading past or riding ponies and rickshaws. The boys were busy spooning away their Tutti Frutti and I was having a cup of coffee. They make it well at the Carlton, with fresh South Indian coffee beans. Frank and I used to come here when we were in language school to splurge a little. For a small town like this it's a fancy restaurant but anywhere else it wouldn't be very special. The waiters are nice. It's clean enough and the Carlton is really the only place in town where you can get a decent cup of coffee.

The boys were still talking about Mr Sing's man-eater. Rev. Turner says there is a leopard on the hillside. I suppose that he should know, since he does a lot of hunting. Rev Turner said that we should be sure to keep Tick inside between dusk and dawn. Last year a leopard took the Keppler's labrador as well as a couple of pariah dogs from the bazaar. It always makes me feel a little uneasy when we walk around at night, and when the boys go out on their beetle-hunting expeditions or down to the stream.

As I was sitting there, drinking my coffee and wondering what I would do if I met a leopard on the path, I noticed two people walking along the mall, a man and a woman. The woman looked very familiar but because of the glare of the sun I couldn't see her until she was almost directly below the window. It was Renuka but the man who was with her I had never seen before. He was quite tall and was wearing an open shirt and khaki shorts. His hair was quite long and he had a beard which gave him a somewhat scruffy appearance. I was surprised to see Renuka with him. They **were** talking together and as they passed by, she put one hand on his shoulder.

Opening the window beside me, I called out to Renuka.

'Hello there,' I shouted.

Renuka stopped and shaded her eyes, looking up at me against the glare of the sun. Her companion had also stopped. The crowds of tourists were swarming around them. Renuka took a moment before she spotted me and then put up her hand and waved.

'Would you like to join us?' I said, raising my coffee cup.

Renuka said something to the man, which I couldn't hear over the noises of the street and then they came up the steps of the restaurant.

'Hello Tim! Hello Michael!' said Renuka, greeting them with her usual enthusiasm and giving each of the boys a kiss.

The bearded man stood awkwardly behind her, looking a little embarrassed. Renuka didn't introduce him at first as she gave me a kiss as well. I finally had to put out a hand.

'Hello, I'm Rachel Manton,' I said.

He took my hand briefly and smiled.

'Amal,' he said.

Renuka turned quickly.

'I'm sorry, I should have done the introductions,' she said. 'Amal is my brother. I told you I had a brother, didn't I?'

I was so surprised, I could only stare at him, seeing the resemblance at once, despite his beard.

'Amal is here on holiday.'

Renuka introduced him to the boys, who had ice-cream dribbling down their chins.

'Rachel is editing a cookbook, a sort of anthology of American home cooking in the Himalayas,' said Renuka. 'She's also the only friend I have in this town.'

'What would you like, a Tutti Frutti or a cup of coffee?' I asked. Renuka slid into the seat next to me and Amal drew up a chair from a nearby table.

'I'll have a Tutti Frutti,' said Renuka, 'I haven't had one since I was in St Marys.'

One of the waiters had come over.

'Would you like one too?' I asked, looking at Amal. I still couldn't get used to the idea that he was Renuka's brother.

'Oh no, just a cup of coffee, please,' he said.

'I've been showing Amal the bazaar, the wonderful, quaint remains of the British empire,' said Renuka, after I had ordered. 'Like all Bengalis, he's a thorough anglophile. We went into a second-hand bookshop, the one near the post office. Amal found two of the most marvellous books on mountain climbing. Why don't you show them what you bought?'

Amal seemed a little overwhelmed by Renuka but he opened his bag and took out two old books that were falling apart at the binding.

'They're quite rare,' he said. 'In Calcutta I would have paid a fortune for these but here they were two rupees each. It's quite a bargain.'

He handed me a thick leather-bound volume, with an ice axe and several coils of rope embossed in gold on the cover.

'That's Tilman's account of his expedition to Kailas, a first edition, and this is an early reprint of Hamilton's famous climb of Vishwa Parbat.'

'Do you collect old books?' I said.

'Yes, especially mountaineering books. It's a hobby of mine.'

'Do you do any mountain climbing?' asked Tim.

'No, I'm afraid not,' said Amal, 'I only read about it.'

The coffee arrived and Renuka's Tutti Frutti. The boys had already finished theirs and I could see that they were getting restless. After a few more minutes I told them that they could be excused.

'Where are the two of you going?' asked Renuka.

'To see a movie,' said Michael.

'What's showing?' asked Amal.

'It's a Jerry Lewis movie,' said Tim, 'I forget the name.'

'I really don't know how they can stand him,' I said. 'He's so ridiculous.'

By then the boys were already out the door.

'But I love Jerry Lewis,' said Renuka. 'How can you not find him funny? He's my favourite comedian.'

Amal looked at her with a cynical expression.

'He always reminds me of a baboon,' he said.

'Well, you've never had a sense of humour anyway,' said Renuka. There was a sharpness to her voice which startled me.

'This is quite a grand hotel,' said Amal, looking around the restaurant. 'It must have been very posh in its day. What's it called?'

'The Carlton,' I said. 'There's even a ball room. At one time it was *the* hotel in town.'

'Their Tutti Frutti's very good,' said Renuka. I could tell that she was a little distracted and seemed to be ignoring her brother on purpose.

'I've always thought that there was something very sad about a place like this,' said Amal. 'It has a romantic atmosphere but so tragic too, as though there's nothing left.'

'I can just imagine what it must have been like with the women all dressed in taffetas and crinolines and the Maharajahs in their brocade coats and turbans,' I said.

'All things must end,' said Amal.

'Stop being so sentimental, both of you,' said Renuka. 'Here Rachel, this is for you?'

She was holding the maraschino cherry from her Tutti Frutti on the end of her spoon.

'No, thank you,' I said, shaking my head.

Giving me an arch look, she popped it in her mouth.

'I've heard they're poisonous,' she said.

After we had finished, Amal said that he wanted to wander around the bazaar for a little while longer, so Renuka decided to walk home with me.

'I can go home by myself,' I said. 'It doesn't matter. If you want to stay with Amal.'

'No, I've had enough of second-hand shops,' said Renuka. 'Amal can find his own way home. Besides, he walks too fast for me. I'd rather go with you.'

I could sense that Renuka was looking for an excuse to get away from him.

The waiter brought our bill and before I could pay it, Amal had picked it up and put a hundred rupee note on the tray.

'Please let me pay,' I said. 'That isn't fair.'

Amal shook his head politely.

'Let him pay,' said Renuka. 'He's a wealthy man.'

I didn't like the way she said it but there was nothing I could do. Renuka was in a rush to leave.

'Come. Let's go,' she said, pulling me by the arm.

It was a strange way for her to act, since he was her brother and she probably hadn't seen him for a long time, but Amal didn't seem to mind. I thanked him and said I hoped we'd meet again.

'Why were you so awful to him?' I said, once Renuka and I were on the street.

She laughed.

'He's such a bore,' said Renuka.

'But you shouldn't have let him pay for everything. I was the one who invited you to come and join us.'

'Don't be silly, Rachel,' she said. 'He's filthy rich. He's got his own advertising company. He'll just put it on his expense account.'

'That doesn't make any difference,' I said.

Renuka looked at me impatiently.

'Oh, come on, don't be such a twit. Amal doesn't mind. After all, I am his sister.'

I was annoyed with her but I was also curious.

'Why didn't you ever tell me you had a brother?' I said.

140

'Because I forgot that he existed,' she said. 'I hadn't heard from him for over a year and suddenly there he was on my doorstep yesterday morning.'

'You weren't expecting him?' I said.

'He says he wrote me a letter but it never reached me. I don't know whether he actually did. He's like that, impulsive, unreliable.'

'A little bit like you,' I said.

'Not at all. Rachel, you're being unfair. Amal is a romantic. He's always been that way. I'm not at all like him.'

'He seems quite nice,' I said.

'Oh, he's absolutely charming,' said Renuka. 'But don't let his manners fool you. He's like most people that have money. They love to take advantage of those who don't. Just imagine. He wants to stay with me for two weeks. It's quite an imposition.'

'But, Renuka, he is your brother,' I said. 'I would have thought you would be glad to see him.'

'Somehow I've become a very private person in my old age. The last thing I need is a house guest.'

'It can't be all that bad,' I said. 'You have an extra room.'

'I admit it's nice to see him again and talk about old times but after a while it wears me down. He's so full of himself.'

'I thought he was interesting.'

'But you're meeting him for the first time. He just goes on and on, the same stories over and over,' said Renuka. 'Besides, he's so demanding.'

'Is he younger than you?' I said.

'No. He's two years older, but he's always looked much younger.' Renuka said this with a spiteful edge to her voice which made me want to laugh.

We passed a line of rickshaws and the coolies called out to us, asking if we wanted a ride. There were tourists all around, dressed up in bright coloured clothes with fur hats on their

heads, the men twirling their walking sticks. The bazaar had
the feeling of a carnival, with balloon sellers and little stalls
along the pavement, selling everything from key chains to
costume jewelry.

'I really can't understand you, Renuka,' I said. 'If one of my
brothers came to visit me, I'd be so happy.'

Renuka blew out her cheeks.

'Yes, but I'm sure your brothers aren't self-absorbed pigs
like mine.'

'You really don't like him, do you?' I said.

'Not if I have to put up with him for more than an hour or
two,' said Renuka. 'Now let's forget about him for the moment,
before I say something really terrible.'

A light rain had started to fall and I opened my umbrella so
that we could share it. Slipping her arm through mine, Renuka
steered me through the crowds of milling tourists.

Somehow I had always thought of Renuka as an only child,
a pampered and protected girl who had run away from home.
There were so many things that she kept hidden from me, so
many secrets. At times it made me feel resentful, as if she was
a puzzle which I was supposed to put together. She would tell
me fragments of her past, throwing out names and incidents
at random. So often, in the middle of a conversation, I would
have to stop her and say, 'Renuka, I don't know who you're
talking about.' She would look at me with a blank expression
and then wave her hand. 'It's not important, just a friend of
mine from Calcutta days. I'm sorry. I thought you knew about
him.' Usually, she would tell me only those things which she
seemed to find amusing and avoided unpleasant topics. I found
it frustrating when Renuka talked about her past because I
wanted to ask her more but she would skip ahead or tell me,
'Rachel, why on earth would you want to know about her? She
was such a cow. And anyway, none of it matters any more.'

142

'But don't you miss Calcutta?' I would say.

'Not at all.'

'You don't think you'll ever go back?'

'Never,' she would say.

Once I asked her why she'd left Calcutta but as usual Renuka dodged the question with a flippant remark. I got a feeling that there had been some kind of family trouble and I didn't think it was any of my business to ask too many questions. Besides, I knew that she would tell me only as much as she wanted to. It wasn't that Renuka was being dishonest or secretive; I think it was because she wanted to live in the present. Still, I couldn't help being curious about her past.

On the wall in her bedroom there was a charcoal sketch of a young woman, just her profile. It was roughly done and one section had been smudged, as if someone had tried to rub it out. At first I thought it was a picture of Renuka herself, as a young girl. The picture intrigued me because it seemed as if she hadn't realized that her portrait was being drawn, the way her face was turned away. In one corner there was something written in Bengali and a date. When I asked Renuka about the picture she told me it was done by a well known artist, who had been a friend of hers.

'He drew it one night at a party, when he was very drunk,' she said. 'It's not a very good likeness. But he did capture that look on Aruna's face, her pensive shyness.'

'I thought it was a picture of you,' I said.

Renuka looked at me with a puzzled expression. Then she laughed, but a little oddly, as though my mistaking it for her portrait had startled her.

'No, of course it isn't me,' she said. 'It's Aruna.'

'Who's Aruna?'

'I've told you about Aruna,' she said, impatiently, 'She was a friend of mine. A poet. I knew her for a while.'

'You've never mentioned her before,' I said.

143

'Of course I have.'

Something in the way she said this made me sense her reluctance to talk about the picture. As with many things, I think she actually believed that she had told me about Aruna, though she had not. It was as if I had touched on something which she didn't want to talk about. Instead, she told me all about the artist and how he'd finally drunk himself to death. The next time I came to the house, I noticed that Renuka had taken the picture down and it was nowhere to be seen.

CHAPTER 11

MINCE TARTS	**Ibrahim Sharif**
ingredients for filling:	ingredients for pastry shells:
1/2 cup raisins	3 cups flour
1/4 cup sultanas	3 eggs
1/4 cup chopped walnuts	1/2 cup shortening
1/4 cup candied peel	1 cup milk
1/2 cup mollases (gur)	2 tablespoons sugar
3 tablespoons plum jam	2 tablespoons melted butter
1 tablespoon ground ginger	

Prepare the pastry shells first by mixing and kneading the ingredients (except butter) together until the dough is a smooth, pliable consistency. Add a little water if needed. Roll out the dough and cut into circles about 6 inches diameter. Use buttered cupcake trays and bake for forty-five minutes at 375 degrees. Remove and allow to cool. Save extra dough for covering tarts. Mix all of the ingredients for the filling together in a large mixing bowl. If sultanas have not been cleaned, remove seeds first. Fill the pastry shells and cutting the remaining dough into strips, cover each one with a criss-cross pattern. Brush on a little butter to give a golden brown colour. Bake for another twenty minutes. Recipe makes two dozen tarts.

I wasn't sure if Ibrahim Sharif, the bread wallah, would be willing to give us his recipe for mince tarts but when I asked him he was quite ready to tell me the ingredients while I wrote them down. He comes around to the house every morning with a Nepali coolie carrying a trunk full of baked goods on his back. I don't usually buy anything from him except for bread and sometimes cookies or peanut brittle. He makes cakes too and all kinds of pastries, most of which are not so good. Ibrahim Sharif is famous on the hillside for his mince tarts, which he makes only as special orders, if someone asks him ahead of time. I usually order a couple dozen just before we go down to Ranchi for the winter holidays so that we can have them at Christmas time. His tarts have a special flavour and they're not as sweet as mince pies usually are.

All of the bakers in town are Muslims and I once asked Ibrahim Sharif how they had come to the hills because most of the local villagers are Hindus. He said that they had been settled here by the British many years ago and originally came from Najibabad. His father had been one of the first to set up a bakery in the bazaar; he used to supply the hotels and the British cantonment with cakes and pastries. Ibrahim Sharif still has letters of recommendation from Britishers who used to buy his father's cakes and bread back in the twenties and thirties. He always carries the letters with him and keeps them folded carefully in a little tin box. When he showed them to me, the letters were almost falling apart, with spidery handwriting in praise of his chocolate eclairs and soda biscuits. Ibrahim Sharif also has more recent letters from missionaries recommending him to others as an honest, dependable baker. There are about four different bread wallahs who come around the hillside and they go from door to door. It's like that with most of the things we buy; there's an egg wallah, a meat wallah, a fish wallah, a milk wallah, a vegetable wallah, and a fruit wallah. Each of them comes to the house and tries to sell me something. I usually let Bindru deal with them, unless I want something special. They're a little bit more expensive than if I bought things from the bazaar but it's much more convenient.

Of all the wallahs that come around Ibrahim Sharif is the nicest. He's a fairly heavyset man and wears a light blue coat and a Kashmiri hat. Even on the clearest day, he carries an umbrella over one arm and looks a little like a comedian with his oversized shoes. He has a white beard that he keeps trimmed close to his cheeks. His way of talking is polite and his manners are very deferential, though there is a dignity about him that sets him apart from the other wallahs.

After he had dictated the recipe, Ibrahim Sharif told me about 'Herschel memsahib' who had gone back to America many years before but always ordered mince tarts from him. She would send him a money order each year and he would despatch two dozen mince tarts to America. I didn't believe him at first but he showed me the postal receipts which he had saved in the same box with his recommendation letters. It was quite touching, I thought, somebody ordering his mince tarts all the way from California.

Before I asked him for the recipe, I warned Ibrahim Sharif that I would be putting it in the cookbook and he should know that if all the women on the hillside learned how to make his tarts, it might put him out of business.

He shook his head and laughed.

'Memsahib, I can give you the recipe, it doesn't matter to me, because I know that even if every memsahib learns how to make mince tarts, they will never be as good as mine.'

Just after I had finished talking to Ibrahim Sharif, I was surprised to see Amal coming down the path. He had brought a note for me from Renuka and seemed a little embarrassed to be delivering it.

'Renuka asked me if I would drop this by,' he said, handing me the note.

'Thank you,' I said. 'Please come inside.'

He sat down on the sofa while I opened the envelope.

147

Dear Rachel,

Forgive this note but I needed an excuse to get my brother
out of the house before I got really irritated with him. Do you
mind looking after Amal for an hour or two? I'm sorry to do
this, Rachel, but he's driving me absolutely crazy. I wish I could
be as patient as you are but he's such an incredible nuisance.

Also, can you come for lunch tomorrow? Please bring something. I think Amal is getting tired of Savitri's dal and rice.

Thank you so much for babysitting.
With love,
Renuka

Somehow, I couldn't get angry with Renuka and I had to
smile at her deception. It was so typical of her to do a thing
like that. I could tell that Amal didn't realize what the note
contained. Renuka could be very wicked sometimes. She was
almost like a child playing surreptitious games. I really couldn't
understand what it was about Amal that bothered Renuka.

'I'd be happy to carry back a reply for you?' he said.

For a moment I didn't know what to say. I'm a terrible liar
and find it hard to keep a straight face.

'Oh, it's not very important,' I said. 'She was just inviting
me for lunch tomorrow.'

'Renuka made it sound as though it was urgent,' he said,
so innocently that I felt guilty deceiving him. Instinctively,
I crumpled up the note, but Amal didn't seem to suspect
anything.

'No, it's nothing urgent,' I said. 'You can tell her that I'll
be happy to come and I'll bring a quiche.'

'Well then, I really should be going,' he said, getting to
his feet.

'No, wait!' I said, quickly.

He looked a little startled by the way I'd spoken.

'I mean. Why don't you stay for tea?' I said.

148

'I didn't know that Americans drank tea,' he said.

'Living in India we've picked up a few bad habits,' I said.

'Are you sure it's no trouble?' he said.

'Of course not,' I said.

Tick had come inside and introduced himself to Amal with his usual, effusive wagging of the tail. I tried to make him stop.

'Don't worry,' said Amal. 'I'm fond of dogs. He's a handsome fellow isn't he?'

'But not very intelligent,' I said.

Asmal was rubbing Tick's ears and scratching him around the neck which made him shiver with delight. I went into the kitchen to ask Bindru to get a tea tray ready and told him to put some cookies on a plate. They were another recipe that I had been trying out for the cookbook, something called peanut butter crackles and not half as bad as I'd expected.

'Are you enjoying your holiday?' I said.

'Very much,' said Amal, 'I haven't been up to the hills for years. When I was a boy, my family usually spent the summers in Darjeeling.'

'It must be very much the same,' I said.

'In some ways,' he said, 'but this hillside is quite unusual, a little corner of America tucked away in the Himalayas.'

'Yes, it must seem very strange to someone who's never been here before.'

'Where is your home in America?' said Amal.

'Minnesota,' I said. 'That's in the centre of the country.'

'I've been to Minneapolis,' said Amal.

'Really?'

'Ten years ago. I went there on a business trip. I remember it was very cold, twenty degrees below zero, they told us. The other thing I remember was the office where we had our meetings, they had this kind of bottled water and you would take a paper cup and it would come out of this little nozzle. It was the best water I've ever tasted.'

'It must have been some kind of spring water,' I said, laughing.

'Whatever it was, I drank about twenty cups. It was so delicious.'

There were moments when I could see Renuka in his face, a clear family resemblance, and I could also hear her in his voice, the way he spoke with such a proper accent, not quite English, but each word pronounced distinctly.

'Do you ever miss America?' asked Amal.

'Sometimes,' I said.

'Renuka says that you've lived in India for quite some time.'

'Twelve years. Almost thirteen.'

'That's a very long time to be away from home,' he said.

'We do go back occasionally.'

'Do you intend to stay here forever?'

'I don't think so,' I said. 'Maybe when the boys finish school, we'll go back.'

'Your husband is a psychologist?'

'A psychiatrist. He runs a mental hospital in Ranchi.'

'He must be a very dedicated man,' said Amal.

For a moment I thought that he was being sarcastic, but then I realized that Amal had meant it seriously. We talked about Ranchi for a while, and Frank's work. Amal seemed interested and asked a lot of questions about the patients and the kind of treatment they were given. The more we talked, the more I liked him. He was not as cynical as Renuka and unlike her, he seemed to listen to what I had to say.

'It must be very difficult living inside a mental home,' said Amal, after I had told him about the compound and our bungalow.

'That's the reason I come up here,' I said. 'To get away.'

150

'Most of the people who live up here, are they missionaries?' he asked.

'Yes,' I said, 'except for Renuka.'

Amal nodded.

'How long have you known my sister?' he said.

'About two years. But we only became close friends last spring.'

'Do you find her eccentric?' he said.

I laughed. 'Sometimes.'

'I may be her brother,' he said, 'but I've never really understood her very well. She's so impulsive, so unpredictable.'

'I guess that's just the way she is,' I said.

Amal paused a moment and gave me an apologetic look.

'Rachel, I am a little concerned about Renuka,' he said. 'I always thought it was a silly thing for her to do, coming up here by herself. It isn't good for her to be alone.'

I didn't say anything, unsure if Amal expected me to agree with him.

'I've been trying to persuade her to come back to Calcutta. She can't go on living as a recluse for the rest of her life.'

'I wouldn't call her a recluse,' I said.

'Not yet, perhaps,' said Amal, 'but other than you, she doesn't seem to have any friends. All she does is sit around in that cottage of hers, brooding like a hen on rotten eggs.'

'I don't think she looks at it like that.'

'Forgive me if I sound over-anxious, but you don't know what she was like in Calcutta. Renuka was lively and sociable, always going to parties, entertaining people at our home, doing interesting things. Everybody loved her. She surrounded herself with intelligent, exciting people, artists, journalists, politicians, everyone from the most decadent poet to the Consul General of Brazil. I can't even begin to describe what she was like, intensely involved in everything she did, always getting into arguments over politics and art. Here she sits like an old

151

widow. I've seen her staring out the window for hours. I hate it, Rachel, I hate to see her so lifeless.'

'Maybe she got tired of being a sociable person. Maybe she needs her privacy,' I said.

'If it was only that,' said Amal, 'I would accept it. I wouldn't try to make her come back. But there's something very sad about Renuka. I know you are her friend and maybe that's why you can't see it in her. I don't know what it is. She's like a ghost.'

'I know that she does get lonely sometimes,' I said, 'but I think she's happy here.'

'Well, perhaps I'm wrong,' said Amal. 'Maybe I'm just being selfish and I want her to come back home.'

Just then the boys arrived from school. Tick heard them coming up the path and shot out of the living room to greet them.

Michael was the first one in. He came bursting through the door, a little out of breath, but stopped suddenly when he saw Amal sitting on the couch.

'Michael,' I said, 'you remember Mr Sen.'

Amal put out his hand and Michael shook it cautiously.

Tim also came inside, carrying a cricket bat. Tick was leaping around in an ecstatic welcome dance.

'Do you play cricket?' said Amal, astonished.

The boys nodded.

'We had a match today,' said Tim.

'Who won?' said Amal.

'The ninth grade. They always do,' said Michael. 'They creamed us.'

The boys helped themselves to the cookies on the plate. Both of them were a little shy at first. Amal asked them about the game and they told him what positions they liked to play and how many runs they'd made. I was glad for the interruption because I wasn't sure what I would say to Amal. I

152

could understand why he was concerned about Renuka but at the same time I felt bad talking about her in this way behind her back.

The boys had finished the cookies before they even sat down. I went out to the kitchen to get some more and when I came back into the room I found Amal showing Michael how to hold the bat a certain way. Tim was standing at the opposite side of the room and at a signal from Amal, he spun the ball at Michael's feet with a flick of his wrist. Michael turned the bat and hit the ball across the living room, so that it banged against the front door. Tick made a frantic dash for it and almost knocked over the tea tray. Seeing that I was watching, Amal and the boys eyed me guiltily.

'I'm sorry, Rachel. I was just showing Michael a trick or two,' said Amal.

I tried to look as disapproving as I could but I wasn't really angry. It was so nice to have a man in the house and to hear the boys talking with him. They got into a long discussion about fast bowling, something to do with the captain of the Indian team. With me they act as though I wouldn't understand the kind of things that interest them. Whenever I ask them questions about cricket or any of their other sports, they just sort of shrug it off and act as though it's not something which concerns me. I know that's part of growing up but it was nice to hear them telling Amal about the hike which they were planning for the coming weekend to Jawala Tibba, one of the nearby peaks. Amal listened to them very seriously, and asked how far it was and how much weight they would be carrying.

We sat and talked for a long time until it was growing dark. I asked Amal whether he would stay for supper but he shook his head.

'I really should be getting back to Erinfell. Renuka must be wondering where I am,' said Amal.

I wanted to laugh and tell him that she was probably enjoying her solitude.

'Thank you for the tea,' he said, getting to his feet. 'And boys, don't forget what I told you about using your wrists.'

'Goodbye,' I said. 'Say hello to Renuka.'

'See you at lunch tomorrow.'

'I'll look forward to that.'

We had just finished dinner and the boys were settling down to do their homework when I heard a knock at the door. I was surprised to see Renuka standing there. At first I was worried that something had happened but she looked quite cheerful and greeted me with a kiss.

'Hello. What brings you here?' I said.

'I just wanted to thank you for looking after Amal this afternoon.'

'Did he get home all right?' I said.

'Yes, I've left him reading about the Nanda Devi expedition of thirty-two, or something equally boring.'

I was surprised that Renuka had come over, especially since she had invited me to lunch the next day. We sat down together in the living room.

'Do you mind if I have a drink?' she said.

'I'm afraid I don't have anything to offer you but coffee,' I said.

'Not to worry. I brought my own.' From out of her handbag, she took a half bottle of rum.

'Will you join me?' said Renuka.

'No thanks, but I'll get you a glass,' I said.

'With some water, please,' she said.

When I brought it for her, she made her drink, pouring the dark rum into the water. It mixed slowly and turned an amber colour. After it was ready, Renuka closed the bottle and took a sip from her glass, grimacing at the taste.

'Horrible stuff,' she said, and smiled. 'Now tell me, what did you and Amal talk about?'

I had a suspicion that was the reason she had come and I couldn't help but feel annoyed with her for playing games like this.

'We talked about different things,' I said.

'Did you talk about me?' she said.

'A little,' I said.

'Well, what did he say?'

'Amal told me that he wants you to go back to Calcutta,' I said. I knew there was no point in trying to evade her questions.

Renuka blew out her cheeks and laughed.

'He keeps on harping about that,' she said. 'I really don't know why.'

'He's worried that you're becoming a recluse,' I said.

'Did he say that?' she said.

I nodded.

'He doesn't understand,' said Renuka. 'He never will. He's always tried to make me do the things he feels are right.'

'Is that why you dislike him so much?' I said.

She was quiet for a moment.

'You don't know my brother,' she said, 'You don't know how shallow and insensitive he can be. Of course he's charming. He learned his manners well in England. Everybody is fooled by him, the way he speaks with such a cultured accent, his handsome face, his gentleness. But Rachel, please believe me when I tell you he's nothing but a fraud.'

'I think you're exaggerating,' I said. 'You may have something against him but I don't know why you have to try and make me hate him too.'

Renuka eyed me over the rim of her glass.

'As a child I used to look up to Amal,' she said. 'He was my idol and I thought that nobody could be as wonderful as

155

my brother. He was good-looking. He was athletic. He was intelligent. Of course, I was blind to all his faults, just like any baby sister. You know how it is, with an older brother. He got all the attention in our family and I suppose the only thing I could do was lavish my affections on him as well. Now that I think of it, he was such a spoiled brat. He was sent to the best schools and my father arranged that he should go to Cambridge. Everything was made available to him while I was shipped off to a miserable little convent in Darjeeling. Despite my father's liberal postures, he didn't believe in wasting money on my education, since he assumed that I would be married off at the age of eighteen.'

She took a drink from her glass and hesitated, as if trying to shake free a memory or rearrange her thoughts.

'I don't think I was ever jealous of Amal. When he was away at Cambridge I used to write him long letters full of all the gossip in our family. He would write back and describe the winters in England, how he and his friends played cricket in the snow and went to the theatre in London. I thought of him as a man of the world with whom I could have conversations about poetry and politics. I remember in one of his letters he had written that he was studying Spencer at college. I went out and bought a collection of his poems just so that I could read them and discuss it with Amal when he returned.

'Rachel, you have to understand, I couldn't care less about the way a person behaves, but with Amal it's always been different because he is my brother. I worshipped him for so many years . . .'

She stopped and held up her empty glass. I went to get her some more water from the kitchen. Though Renuka seemed to be upset, somehow I couldn't feel sorry for her.

'Amal stayed in England for seven years. After he got his degree he worked in London for a while. When he finally wrote and said that he was coming back, all of us were

156

thrilled. I expected him to be dressed like Sherlock Holmes with a pipe in his mouth, a proper gentleman. Everyone was excited and my father even had the house repainted for his return. He had gone to England by sea but he came back by air. We all went to receive him and I remember watching the plane coming in to land and holding my breath as it taxied up to the terminal.

'There was great excitement and celebration when Amal got home. He had brought all kinds of gifts for us, and in the evening he told us that he had an important announcement to make. We were all in the sitting room and suddenly Amal got very serious. I was puzzled. He seemed a little nervous. Without looking anyone in the eye, he told us he was married. He had an English wife. Her name was Bethany and she was coming to Calcutta in another week.

'You should have seen my parents' faces. In his letters he hadn't told us anything about her, even though they'd been married for three years. Amal tried to explain that he thought it would be less of a shock if he told us face to face. My mother started to cry and my father was so angry that he couldn't say a word. Even I was upset with him. What bothered me most of all was that he had deceived us. For three years, he had kept it secret and pretended that he was a bachelor. Now, when we were all celebrating his return, he sprung it on us like a cruel surprise.

'Rachel, I was so disheartened, not because I cared whether he was married or not, or even that he had an English wife. It just seemed so tactless. Here I had waited all these years for my brother to come back and now he looked so foolish, so cowardly, so simple-minded.

'Bethany arrived the following week and by that time we had recovered enough to hide our disappointment. She was a short and blowsy woman with reddish hair and an unhappy squint. I went with Amal to the airport and all she could talk

157

about on the way back home was the pastries they had served her on the plane.

'You're probably thinking I was jealous of her, Rachel. But truly she was so disgusting, a real English wench. She had a coarse East London accent and she wore the most appalling clothes. I couldn't stand her. I tried to be her friend but it was impossible. All she could talk about was her family. Her parents lived in Brighton and owned a pub. I really don't know where my brother met her and I thought it better not to ask. She mispronounced his name so badly and called him "Sweets" which made me cringe. Of course, he was her slave.

'We were all living together in my parents' house, an old victorian mansion which was built by my great grand uncle. My mother and father had their rooms downstairs and Amal and his wife took over the upper floor. I was moved out to the annexe at the back, which was actually a relief because I didn't have to deal with them. We ate our meals together, though, and it was awfully painful for me. Bethany told us that she wanted to become like us, "a real Bengali" but she was always worried about the chillies in the food and Amal had to boil her water separately. She got sick so often it seemed as though Amal was always taking her to the doctor.

'Four or five months after she arrived, Bethany got pregnant which made her even more intolerable, swelling up like a balloon. I watched it all as if it were a farce, and even from the start I knew their marriage was doomed. The child was born after a hysterical week in which she went into false labour three days in a row and had to be rushed to the hospital each time. You really wouldn't have believed the sort of dramatics she put on and Amal looked so anxious. In the end, they had a boy, which delighted everyone but me. I think I would have been happiest if she'd given birth to a calf. He was a little snot-nosed boy, as spoiled and silly as his father.'

Renuka stopped and poured herself another rum. This time she took no water and I could tell that she was getting drunk.

'After their son came into the house, I really couldn't stand it any more. He was always wailing and his mother used to bring him out into the courtyard and roll him about in a pram just beneath my bedroom window. One day I asked her to take him inside because his crying was disturbing me. She got offended and told Amal who came and gave me a scolding as if it were my fault. Amal accused me of being insensitive. I told him he was one to talk, the way he'd brought her into the household and expected all of us to be pleasant and understanding. He didn't seem to realize how difficult it was for my parents. They felt so awkward with Bethany around and even though they loved the baby, I think that all of us wished that Amal would take his family back to England.

'In the middle of all this my father died quite suddenly from a heart attack. Amal had to perform the last rites. Relatives came from here and there. All of us were supposed to be in mourning but there was Bethany, dressed up in her brightest clothes, parading her pram up and down the street. During one of the prayer sessions after my father's death she even played her rock and roll records upstairs, so loud that we could hear it in the sitting room. She was totally unaware of the way she offended people. One of my uncles had come to stay with us and he was a very dignified man but he had a way of curling his lips when he spoke that made Bethany laugh out loud. She couldn't control herself and it was so embarrassing.

'By this time, she was getting bored. The novelty of Calcutta had worn off and she'd made friends with one or two other British women, typical expatriates. They would get together almost every day and complain about India, how it was so impossible to live here, all the problems, flies, rats, poverty, the power shortages. Their list was endless and they seemed to think they were the only ones that suffered.

'My mother got so tired of Bethany she wouldn't even acknowledge that she was in the same room. Things were heading towards a crisis and I could tell that even Amal had started to realize his mistake. The final blow was really rather pathetic, the sort of minor skirmish that leads to war.

'Bethany had gone out to a tea party with her English friends and left her son at home. He was almost a year old by then and crawling all about. They had hired an ayah to look after him and wash his clothes, a slovenly, untidy woman whom none of us liked. I was writing letters in my apartment at the back, when I heard a crashing sound. Going into the house I found the baby, his name was Roger, sitting in the middle of the floor surrounded by broken glass. He had tipped over one of the full length mirrors which stood at either end of the dining room and it had shattered. Thankfully, he wasn't hurt at all but looked a little dazed. I picked him up and by that time the ayah had appeared.

'I shouted at her for being so careless and told her it was all her fault. My mother came out of her room and when I explained what had happened, she immediately told the ayah she was dismissed. I know it was a drastic thing to do but we were all quite shaken and the woman had been very irresponsible. Neither Amal nor Bethany was at home. Of course the ayah got into a huff and since it was the first of the month and she had just been paid, the wretched woman packed her things and left.

'All of this happened before Bethany came home but when she did, she wasn't so upset that Roger had nearly been killed but that we had sacked the ayah. She acted as if we had no right to do a thing like that. Bristling with indignation, she said that we should have consulted with her first. Taking Roger, who was asleep by then, she marched upstairs. Amal returned a

160

little later and he walked into a hornet's nest. My mother was irate and kept saying it was still her house and she would hire and fire the servants as she wished.

'Upstairs Amal must have got the other side of the story. Finally he came to me and tried to get some sympathy. I told him what I'd seen, the baby sitting in the middle of the room with shards of glass all around him while the ayah was outside gossiping with her friends. I said that there was every reason for the woman to be sacked, and for once Amal admitted that I was right. He returned upstairs and must have tried to be firm with Bethany but all I could hear was her voice, shrill and tearful. She went on and on like a loudspeaker and I could imagine all of her complaints, blaming Amal, accusing us of hating her. She wailed and shouted for hours.

'The next morning when I saw Amal he looked distraught and tired. I asked him how things were and without looking at me he said that she was leaving. I shouldn't have done it but I couldn't help saying, 'How soon?' He said that Bethany had called one of her English friends, whose husband worked for BOAC, and they were going to get her onto a London flight that evening. Amal didn't appreciate it when I offered to help her pack but I think that in the end he was as relieved as all of us. A taxi came and took her away along with Roger and his pram. We didn't say goodbye, though I watched her leaving from the window.

'I know it must sound as though I was heartless and unsympathetic, Rachel, but really, that woman was impossible and once she left, I was so relieved.'

'She didn't come back?' I said.

'No chance of it,' said Renuka. 'After about a year, they got a divorce. Amal had to go to London but she wouldn't let him see their son. I thought that was unnecessarily cruel. Amal was upset for quite a while but he seems to have pulled himself together.'

'It must have been awful,' I said.

'Worse than that,' said Renuka. 'It was hell.'

Taking a last drink from her glass she got to her feet. Renuka seemed quite steady, though her eyes were glazed and I had to help her open the front door. When I asked if she needed a torch, Renuka shook her head.

'Cat's eyes, Rachel,' she said. 'I can see things in the dark that aren't even there.'

CHAPTER 12

QUICHE	Dorothy Monkman
4 eggs	1/2 cup grated cheese
3 tablespoons milk	1/2 teaspoon basil
2 tablespoons butter	1/2 teaspoon thyme
3 strips bacon, finely chopped	1/2 teaspoon salt

Beat eggs, milk and butter together. Add cheese, salt and spices and pour into a pie crust (see recipe p. 32). Sprinkle bacon over the top and bake for half an hour at 350 degrees or until top of the quiche turns a light brown. Serve hot or cold.

I had been wanting to try Dorothy Monkman's quiche recipe for some time but knew that the boys would never eat it. Bindru is very good at making pie crust so I let him do that part and then showed him how to make the filling. He couldn't quite get used to the idea of a salty pie and asked me several times what kind of fruit I was going to use. He gets that worried look sometimes when I'm working in the kitchen as though he thinks I'm doing everything wrong but doesn't have the nerve to tell me. He's been having a lot of trouble with his eyes and last week I sent him to the hospital with a note. Dr Foster says his cataracts need to be operated on but Bindru refuses to have it done. He's afraid that he'll go completely blind.

After my conversation with Renuka the night before, I didn't feel like going to Erinfell for lunch. The last thing I wanted was to get caught in the middle of a family squabble. I had been disturbed by what she'd told me about Amal's wife, and I couldn't imagine him married to a woman like that. The more I thought about it, the more I realized that Renuka had told me only a part of the truth.

When I reached Erinfell, a few minutes past noon, I saw Amal sitting outside, under the apricot tree with a book in his hand. Renuka was nowhere in sight.

Seeing me coming down the path, Amal raised one hand and waved. He closed his book and got out of the chair to meet me. I was holding the quiche pan in one hand, tied up in a dishtowel.

'So, you've brought us lunch?' said Amal.

'It's just a quiche,' I said. 'I hope you like it.'

'I love quiche. Is this something from your cookbook?' he asked.

'Yes,' I said. 'Though it isn't my recipe.'

'You know, I pretend to be something of a cook myself,' he said.

'Really?' I said.

'Nothing very fancy of course, but eatable.'

'Maybe you can give me a recipe,' I said.

'Oh, I don't use recipes,' he said. 'I work on inspiration. You know a pinch of this and a dash of that.'

'I'm not used to meeting a man who admits that he can cook,' I said.

'Well, I can make a tolerable stew,' said Amal, 'and I'm rather good at making omelettes.'

'Where's Renuka?' I said.

'She's having a bath. I'll take that in and give it to Savitri. Can I get you a glass of beer?'

I was about to refuse and then I thought, why not?

'Yes, please,' I said.

Amal carried the quiche into the kitchen and returned a few minutes later with two glasses of beer.

'I enjoyed talking with your boys yesterday,' he said. 'You must be very proud of them.'

'I guess I am.'

'How old are they?'

'Michael is nine and Tim is eleven.'

'I have a son who's ten,' he said.

'Renuka told me.'

'Did she also tell you that I'm divorced?'

'Yes, I'm sorry.'

He started to laugh. 'No reason for you to be sorry,' he said.

'I meant it must be very hard to be separated from your son,' I said.

'Yes, it is,' he said. 'I haven't seen him since he was a year old.'

'Is he in England?' I said.

Amal nodded and looked away.

'Forgive me,' I said, 'I didn't mean to pry.'

'You aren't prying,' he said, taking a swig of his beer. 'It's just the way things are.'

From the yard of Renuka's house we had a clear view of the snow peaks, and though it was a hazy day there were no clouds. I am so used to seeing the mountains but they still give me a feeling of awe when I look out at them, the stark white façade and jagged profiles. I had noticed that the book which Amal had been reading was one of those which he had bought in the bazaar.

'Are any of these mountains mentioned in your book?' I said.

'No, I don't think you can see Kailas from here. It's further back,' he said, picking up the book. 'This is quite a wonderful story, though. In those days everything was fairly basic, no nylon ropes or aluminium poles. They really climbed the mountain on its own terms. None of these oxygen tanks and lightweight tents.'

'I've never understood why anyone would want to climb a mountain,' I said. 'It's so much nicer just to look at them from here.'

'But it must give you a certain feeling of exhilaration to be standing up there on top of the world,' said Amal, thoughtfully. 'I can imagine the excitement, though I probably wouldn't want to do it myself. Can you believe, they got caught in a storm and had to spend four days inside their tents with the wind blowing around them and their food frozen solid.'

'No, thank you,' I said, shuddering at the thought.

'And then they lost half of their supplies down a crevasse. It's quite unbelievable the things that they endured.'

'Did they finally get to the top?' I asked.

'Oh yes,' he said. 'though two of them died on the way down, in an avalanche.'

'It's hard to imagine. The mountains look so peaceful from here, not dangerous at all.'

For a moment, we both kept staring at the snows.

'You're not drinking any of your beer,' said Amal.

'I'm really not used to it,' I said. 'I hardly ever drink. Only when I'm with Renuka.'

'She's corrupted you,' he said.

'Not really.'

'Sometimes I think she's a bad influence on people,' said Amal.

Renuka still hadn't come out from her bath and I was wondering how long she would take. Maybe she was doing it on purpose, just to have a little time to herself. Amal and I kept talking. He told me more about the book and made me finish my glass of beer and went to get another. I tried to say 'no' but he told me that there was nothing wrong with a little beer in the afternoon.

166

'Have you read any of Renuka's poems?' he asked.

'Some,' I said.

'I remember she wrote a play once. It was very good, something about a woman who has an imaginary tiger for a pet. I think it was called, "The Fur Coat". My memory isn't very good but at the end of the play this woman's husband buys her a fur coat as a present and she begins shouting at him and accuses him of killing her pet.'

'It sounds very strange,' I said.

'Well, the whole thing was quite modern and a little abstract but we did a dramatic reading of it at one of the theatres in Calcutta. Everyone who came to the reading thought it was splendid.'

Just then, Renuka appeared on the verandah. I was surprised to see that she was wearing a sari. Her hair was still wet from her bath and she had brushed it out so that it covered her shoulders. She was full of apologies.

'I'm so sorry, Rachel, the damned hot water ran out before I could wash my hair and I had to wait for another bucket to heat. Amal must think we live such primitive lives,' she said.

'On the contrary,' he said, 'I don't think there's anything more civilized than sitting under an apricot tree with the Himalayas in the distance and two beautiful women to talk with.'

'Stop being so charming and get me a beer,' said Renuka, sharply.

Amal didn't seem bothered by her tone of voice and went off to the kitchen. Renuka sat down beside me.

'I'm sorry I took so long,' she said, softly, 'I hope that Amal hasn't been too boring?'

'He's been very nice.'

Renuka laughed and looked at me with a mischievous expression. Neither of us mentioned her visit of the night before. She threw back her head and then leaned forward so that her hair fell down over her face. Renuka brushed it away from the nape of her neck and I could see that the shoulders of her blouse were wet.

'I've been thinking of cutting my hair,' said Renuka. 'What do you think?'

'Don't,' I said, 'You've got the most beautiful hair I've ever seen. I'd never forgive you if you cut it.'

'I was thinking of cutting it very short with a wedge on one side,' she said. 'Do you think it would suit me?'

'I think your hair looks very nice as it is.'

She was leaning forward, letting the sun fall on the back of her neck and brushing her hair steadily.

'But it's such a lot of trouble,' said Renuka. 'I'm always having to fuss with it and on a day like this when the water runs out, I just feel like taking a pair of scissors and chopping it off.'

Amal had returned with the glass of beer for Renuka. He set it down on the garden table beside her. Renuka quickly raised her head and gathered her hair behind her neck into a loose hank which she twisted once and knotted.

'What do you think, Amal?' she said. 'Should I cut my hair?'

'Absolutely not,' he said.

'You're both the same. You don't have any imagination,' she said. 'Can't you understand that I'm enslaved to my hair? I'm tied to it. I just wish sometimes that during the night somebody would steal into my room and chop it off. I want to wake up one morning and find it gone, all shorn.'

'When did you last cut it?' I asked.

'In school. I used to have very long hair as a child and the nuns would make me spend hours oiling and braiding it. I hated to have it tied in ribbons and they would make me pin it up like mickey mouse ears. Do you remember, Amal, how you used to tease me about it? One day, I stole a pair of scissors

168

from Sister Evangeline's drawer and went into the bathroom. I cut off each braid, just like that, snip . . . snip. It was so easy. The braids fell to the floor like a pair of snakes and there I was. Of course, my hair looked very strange with two tufts on either side and when Sister Evangeline saw me, she screamed. Afterwards they tried to make me tell them what I'd done with my hair but I wouldn't say a word. I buried it in a flower pot behind the grotto in the garden. I wouldn't tell them where it was because I was afraid that they would pin it back on again. Anyway, everyone was very angry and Mother Josephine wrote to my parents. When I went home for the holidays, I looked like a boy, which suited me all right but my mother was furious and since then I've never cut it again.'

Renuka seemed more at ease and she stopped being rude to Amal. He asked her if the nuns had ever tried to make her a Christian.

'Not really,' she said. 'They would give me holy pictures sometimes and little charms to hang around my neck, but they knew that I would never be a good Catholic.'

Renuka winked at me. There was none of the tension and bitterness between her and Amal which I had expected. They actually seemed to be enjoying each other's company. It made me feel a little silly and I wondered if I had imagined everything from the night before. Renuka had seemed so upset and angry with her brother but now they were talking happily, as if nothing was wrong.

'So, Rachel, how is the cookbook coming along?' asked Renuka.

'Slowly,' I said, 'I'm getting a lot of recipes but it's hard to choose which ones I want. We're having a potluck supper on Friday night. Everybody's supposed to bring something and there are going to be judges to choose the prize-winning recipes.'

'Am I allowed to enter?' said Renuka.

'Of course. If you really want to. I think it's going to be a bit of a disaster, to tell the truth,' I said. 'I just don't like the idea of a cooking competition.'

'It must be a lot of work for you, being the editor,' said Amal.

'It is,' I said.

'But Rachel is so good at that sort of thing,' said Renuka. 'She's so organized.'

'That isn't true,' I said.

'But you are,' said Renuka. 'Whenever I come to your house, I'm always amazed how orderly it is, everything in its place. Look at my house, on the other hand. Amal must think I never put anything back where it belongs.'

'Don't be silly,' said Amal. 'You've got a wonderful house.'

'I think so too,' I said.

'The problem is that I keep collecting things,' said Renuka. 'Sometimes I feel like getting rid of everything, the furniture, the books, my bed, my pictures. It would be so nice to have absolutely no possessions. I still remember how wonderful it was when I first got here. The house was all bare and freshly white-washed. It was so empty, I hated to begin unpacking and I almost wished that all my luggage had been lost.'

'But you have so many valuable things. Your statues. Your paintings,' I said.

'They may be worth a lot of money but I don't know whether I can really think of them as valuable. Those paintings used to belong to my father and I have looked at them since childhood. The statues I bought years ago from an old Burmese woman who needed money. I got them for next to nothing and it's always made me feel guilty, as if I cheated her. I know they're beautiful works of art but after all these years, they've become so meaningless.'

'You're not really serious, are you?' I said.

'She's always serious,' said Amal.

'One of the first things I did when I arrived up here, was to burn everything I'd ever written,' said Renuka, her voice subdued.

'That's terrible,' said Amal. I could tell he was actually shocked that Renuka would have done such a thing.

'It was winter and I was sitting in front of the fireplace with the oak logs blazing. I had brought three trunks full of papers from Calcutta and I was sorting through them. It was so depressing that I began to put the papers in the fire, page by page. You don't know what pleasure it gave me. It was as though I were cremating myself, a whole pyre of poems, plays and stories. There were so many of them that the grate got choked with ash and I had to let the fire die down and clean it out. It took me the whole day to burn it all but there was a wonderful feeling at the end.'

'And you have no copies left?' said Amal.

'None. Actually, it was the most intelligent thing I've ever done. I really needed to start all over again.'

'What about that play you wrote, "The Fur Coat"?' said Amal.

'Everything,' she said.

'Your journals too?'

She nodded.

'When I came up here I wanted to forget everything,' she said. 'I wanted to erase my life and start again. I think I understand why sadhus renounce the world and give up all their material possessions.'

For a moment the three of us just sat there in silence, imagining that fire, the sheets of paper turning into flames.

I was glad when Renuka suggested that we go inside for lunch. Savitri had set the table and my quiche lay in the centre along with a salad. The beer had made me drowsy. I excused myself and went into the bathroom to splash some water on my face. When I came out, I heard

171

Amal and Renuka arguing. They were speaking in Bengali, so I couldn't understand what they were saying but Renuka seemed especially angry. I hesitated before going into the dining room but there was no escaping the situation. As I came in, Renuka was gesturing wildly with one hand and shouting at Amal. Seeing me, she stopped. We stared at each other for a moment.

'Forgive us, Rachel,' said Renuka. 'Come. Sit down.'

Though the fight had stopped as abruptly as it began, I could feel Renuka holding back her temper. I cut and served the quiche, and by the time I had finished, Amal seemed to have recovered. He asked me whether the boys were still going on their hike and we talked about them for a while, trying to pretend nothing had happened. Renuka kept very quiet and nibbled at her quiche, not really eating. Once or twice I said something to her and she responded with only a nod of her head. It was as if we were waiting for her to explode again.

'The boys have become so independent now,' I said. 'They don't seem to need me any more.'

'I'm sure that isn't true,' said Amal. 'They're just at the age when they're testing their limits.'

I heard Renuka laugh. 'Since when have you become an expert on children?' she said.

'I was a boy once,' he said, 'I remember what it was like. I used to want to ride the trams on my own when I was ten but my parents wouldn't let me, so I used to sneak out and do it anyway. One time I got lost for several hours.'

'You were a spoiled brat,' said Renuka.

Amal ignored her.

'Have you ever been to Calcutta, Rachel?' he said.

'No,' I said, trying not to look at Renuka.

'It's a wonderful city,' he said.

'It's a dead city,' said Renuka.

'Dying maybe,' said Amal, 'but far from dead.'

'It's a hole,' said Renuka. 'A black, black hole.'

'But there's such a lot happening. People actually go to the theatre and there are dozens of little film societies and coffee shops where artists meet. I know it's grimy and filthy but the city still has character and energy.'

'What bullshit!' said Renuka. 'Sometimes I think you don't have any sense of reality. How can you call it a city? That place is a slum, a refuse heap. You should see the rats in Calcutta, Rachel, as big as man-eating tigers. Don't listen to him. He's talking shit.'

'But don't you miss it sometimes?' said Amal.

'Never,' said Renuka.

'Not even the maidan, with all the kites at dusk?'

Renuka shook her head impatiently.

'What about the sweet shops?' said Amal. 'Don't you miss your mishti? One time you ate fifteen rasogolla at one sitting. You haven't eaten sweets, Rachel, unless you've come to Calcutta.'

'Rachel doesn't like sweets, anyway,' said Renuka.

'I do,' I said, but she wasn't listening to me.

'You're never going to get me to go back to your bloody city,' said Renuka, pushing back her chair and getting to her feet. 'You're such a bastard Amal, such a fucking bastard. I just wish you'd stop harassing me.'

'What do you mean?' said Amal.

'You're trying to get Rachel on your side. That's what you're doing,' she said, her voice rising.

'Please don't shout,' said Amal.

'I'll do anything I like. This is my house, not yours. You can't tell me what to do.'

'Renuka,' I said.

'Don't listen to him, Rachel. He's a liar.'

173

She stood there looking at us wildly for a moment and then threw down her napkin, went into her bedroom and slammed the door.

'I'm sorry,' said Amal.

'I think I should go home,' I said.

'I'll walk you back,' said Amal.

'No,' I said. 'No, thank you.'

I was shaking when I got outside and felt like crying, but at the same time I was angry with Renuka for making such a scene. I felt awful, as if she had used me to get back at Amal. There was something pathetic about the way she yelled at him, as though he frightened her. I could sense the panic in her voice. Earlier she had been so calm and relaxed and then all of a sudden her mood had changed, as if a fuse inside of her had burst.

I didn't see Renuka or Amal for the next two days. There were so many things happening at once. I had to get ready for the cookbook potluck and the boys were all excited about their hike. One of their teachers, George Mullin, was taking a group of them. It was the first long hike that either of the boys had been on and they would be away for two nights. I helped them organize their rucksacks and had to repack everything because Michael had put in six shirts while Tim hadn't packed any at all. I also had to find their sleeping bags and canteens which were locked away in the godown. George Mullin had given them a list of things to bring, two tins of baked beans and a packet of powdered milk, matches, cups, plates and spoons. Michael was also meant to bring a frying pan and Tim was to carry a kettle. I couldn't help feeling a little worried about the two of them but they seemed to be so eager to be going.

Since it was a long weekend they were able to leave on Friday morning. I saw them off at six thirty, both of them with their rucksacks bulging and Michael worried that he already had a blister. They looked like two prospectors setting off to explore the Yukon. Tick was very disappointed that he couldn't go with them and whined until they were out of sight.

It gave me a peculiar feeling to be alone in the house, even though I knew it was only for a weekend. In some ways I was looking forward to being by myself but at the same time the house felt empty and deserted without the boys.

CHAPTER 13

MOUSSAKA	Carla Vorhies
2 large eggplants	1/2 tsp thyme
2½ cups mince meat	1/2 tsp rosemary
1 tsp butter	1 clove crushed garlic
2/3 cups chopped onions	2/3 cup bouillon
1 cup mushrooms	3 tbs tomato paste
1 tsp vinegar	3 eggs
1 tsp salt	1 cup grated cheese
1/2 tsp pepper	

Remove stems and skins of eggplant. Cut into slices lengthwise. Brown onions and mushrooms in butter. Add meat and all other ingredients except eggplant and cheese. Mix thoroughly. Fill a deep casserole with layers of sliced eggplant and remaining ingredients. Bake covered at 375 F for one hour. Sprinkle grated cheese over top and bake until golden brown.

The prize-winning entry at the cookbook potluck was Carla Vorhies' Moussaka. I never got a chance to taste it because it was all finished by the time I served myself and besides, I've never been very fond of eggplant.

I didn't really want to have the cookbook potluck in the first place but Esther Rainey had insisted and the other women on the committee seemed to think it was a good idea. The problem is we seem to have potluck suppers so often and there's always more food than anybody could possibly eat. The whole thing becomes such a mish-mash of different tastes. Just the sight of all that food is enough to make me lose my appetite but because I feel as though I have to be polite, I try to take a taste of everything and end up eating too much and feeling sick. The other thing I don't like about potluck suppers is the way women try to out-do each other and the dishes get more and more elaborate.

Esther was the one who felt that we should have a panel of judges and award prizes for the five best recipes, so that we can put a star beside them in the cookbook. I tried to talk her out of it but she can be so stubborn. As the date for the potluck approached, I began to dread it even more and wished that I had vetoed the idea from the start. As usual, I ended up doing all the dirty work of sending out instructions and making sure that everybody knew the rules. Esther volunteered to pick the judges, which was a big relief, though I didn't completely trust her choice. I could tell that she was planning to stage a coup; and, of course, her chicken gumbo won the second prize.

I got to the Community Centre ahead of time but a lot of women were already there, nervously arranging their dishes on the tables, adding a last garnish to their specialties. I had made a cheese and spinach casserole, one of Frank's favourites. More than ever, I wished that he was there. I know he hates this kind of thing and always ends up in a terrible mood when he has to go to potluck suppers. Even then it would have been nice to have him beside me and know that at least somebody would eat my casserole.

The confusion of the potluck was putting me on edge. All I wanted to do was go back home. Midge Thompson cornered me as I put my casserole on the table. She was in a flap about the decorations being spoiled because her chowkidar had brought pink streamers instead of yellow and they didn't match the table cloths. I told her everything looked fine. Then Esther Rainey made her entrance, with a coolie carrying a huge basket full of fresh bread rolls on his back and an enormous pot of chicken gumbo. Esther came across and kissed me on the cheek, smelling of yeast and hair spray. She told me that Rev. Turner, Dr Carlton and one of the new teachers at the school, Ed Curley had agreed to be the judges. There weren't that many single men on the hillside to choose from and Esther felt that husbands couldn't be trusted to be impartial.

Even though I had arranged everything ahead of time, there was a lot for me to do, especially with Esther interfering and changing things around. All the dishes were set out on tables along one wall. Each of us had taped our names to the bottom of the dishes and there were numbers to go with every recipe so there would be no favouritism amongst the judges. (Esther said that Dr Carlton was soft on Mary Bettman and was sure to choose her egg rolls).

As I was making sure that there were enough water glasses and checking on the punch for the children, someone came and tapped me on the shoulder. Turning around I saw Ted and Connie Simpson standing there. It took me a moment to react.

'Hello, Rachel,' said Connie. 'Look who arrived last night.'

She was beaming and holding Ted by the arm as if she would never let him go.

'Welcome,' I said, as Ted leaned down to give me a kiss.

'How's Frank?' he said.

'He's fine. Still down in Ranchi,' I said, making a disappointed face.

'Ted's going to stay up for a couple of months,' said Connie. 'He's got some reports to write.'

'That's wonderful,' I said.

'Rachel was so helpful when I had the blues,' said Connie, looking up at Ted. He seemed embarrassed. Their daughter Cynthia was playing on the other side of the room with some other children. Ted asked me how the boys were doing and I told them about the hike. Years ago Connie, Ted and Frank and I went on a hike to Jawala Tibba and Ted still remembered how I sprained my ankle and limped all the way back.

'By the way,' said Connie, after we'd been talking, 'Sheba's going to have puppies.'

'Oh no!' I said.

'She sneaked out somehow, just for an hour, but that was long enough.'

After everyone had gathered, Esther got up on the stage and clapped her hands for silence. She made a few announcements and then asked Rev Turner to say the blessing. There was an empty hush, as everyone fell silent. He took a moment before he began. It was a longer prayer than usual and I didn't think it was necessary for him to list the European heads of state for divine guidance or even the three American astronauts who were orbiting overhead that night. The children were getting restless by the time he ended and the "Amen" was like a heart-felt sigh of relief. The judges served themselves first, trying to look judicious as they filled their plates, taking a small portion from each dish. Then they went and sat on three chairs which had been placed aside for them and began to eat while the mothers with small children followed and then the rest in eager succession. The last thing I wanted to do was eat, so I waited until the end to serve myself.

Renuka had said that she would be coming, but I didn't really expect her to turn up, especially not after what happened the other day. Even though I knew everybody in the room, I felt like a stranger lost in a crowd of women I had never met before. One or two of them came up to me, asking questions about the cookbook or making small talk and though I spoke with them there seemed to be nothing much to say.

I noticed Lois Keck sitting in one corner with two of the other Mennonite women. They were talking in lowered tones, adding a sober, almost melancholy presence to the evening in their dour grey dresses. And then there was Isabel Kimberly the new Methodist lady who runs an exercise class every Wednesday morning. She is so thin, her arms look like bread sticks and she never seems to sit still, always jittering around. Last week she gave me a recipe for Granola — she seems to have a thing about health foods. She's only been in India for three months and I had to point out to her that she wasn't going to be able to get some of the ingredients, like wheat germ. Isabel was talking to Ruth Bishop, who's a little overweight and I imagine she was trying to convince her on the benefits of skipping rope. Isabel has been trying to get me to join her class but I told her that I get enough exercise walking up and down the hill.

The younger children were running about the room, weaving through our legs and screaming, while their mothers tried to serve them plates of food that they were sure to waste. I wished that Tim and Michael were with me but I knew that even if they'd come to the potluck, they would have spent the whole time out on the playground with their friends. I wondered how they were doing on their hike and whether they'd got rained on. After they left I noticed that Michael had forgotten his poncho. Anyway, they're old enough to take care of themselves.

I was standing near the bulletin board when Alice Murphy came over and complimented me on my dress. I didn't tell her that it was almost ten years old. She is always complimenting me on my hair, my shoes, my boys. I don't know what it is but she feels as though she has to say something nice to me every time we meet. The problem is that there isn't much that I can say in return because she always looks like such a mess and it would be an obvious lie if I complimented her. That may sound cruel but it is the truth. She has to be the most unattractive woman on the hillside. Fortunately tonight she was wearing an old brooch, which I admired. Of course, when I looked at it closely several stones were missing and I could tell that it was made of brass, but she seemed genuinely pleased that I had noticed the brooch.

The judges had started seconds and Esther stood triumphantly beside her depleted mountain of bread rolls, urging people on like a hawker at a railway platform. I realized that I should serve myself to be polite, even though the sight of all that food was making me feel sick. I took a little salad and Esther spooned a dollop of gumbo onto my plate along with a bread roll. By now the conversation had reached a desperate pitch. It was hard to believe that anyone was eating with all that talk.

I had just taken a bite when Amal walked in. He stood in the doorway, looking slightly lost and bewildered. In his hand he was carrying a small container. I hurried across the room.

'Rachel,' he said, 'I'm so embarrassed. Renuka told me that this was starting at seven o'clock.'

'It doesn't matter,' I said. 'Come in. Where's Renuka?'

'She sends her apologies. I hope it's all right for me to come alone?'

'Of course. I'm so glad you're here.'

I took the container he'd brought and set it on one of the tables.

'That's carrot halva,' said Amal, 'Savitri cooked it up this afternoon.'

'You didn't need to bring anything,' I said. 'There's tons of food, as you can see. Here, let me get you a plate.'

As Amal made his way through the line, serving himself from the different dishes, I could tell that the women around us had noticed him and were beginning to whisper amongst themselves. Amal was wearing a grey tweed jacket and with his beard he looked quite distinguished. It was such a relief to have him there and I felt as though the evening might actually turn out all right.

'Which is yours?' he said.

'It's over there,' I said. 'It's just a cheese and spinach casserole.'

Amal found my dish and took a generous serving.

'It looks wonderful,' he said.

Once he'd filled his plate, we went across and sat down together near the windows. Most of the women were standing in little clusters, talking with their mouths full as though they hadn't seen each other for months. As they caught sight of Amal, I would see them stop in mid-sentence as though something was stuck in their throats. I knew that they'd be saying all kinds of things behind my back but I didn't really care. Jo Tyson was sitting across the room, looking as swollen as ever, and I could see her glancing at us out of the corner of her eye. It didn't matter what they thought, I was glad that Amal was there to save me from all their silly chatter.

'Your casserole is very good,' said Amal, 'but what in God's name is this?'

He was picking at a yellowish blob on his plate.

'I think it's meant to be a jello salad,' I said.

'It has raisins in it,' said Amal.

'Don't eat it if you don't like it,' I said.

'It tastes dreadful,' said Amal, very softly.

Both of us began to laugh. I couldn't control myself. Amal flipped the salad about with his fork and it wiggled across his plate.

'I think it's actually alive,' he said.

Amal kept wobbling the jello and making it squirm. I felt like a schoolgirl sharing a joke in class and trying to keep from laughing.

'Here, put it on my plate,' I said. 'I'm finished.'

'Be careful, it may be poisonous,' he said, sliding it off with his fork.

I wondered whose salad it was and hoped that none of the women around us had made it.

After the potluck supper Amal walked me home. We were amongst the last to leave, since I had to make sure that things got closed up at the Community Centre. Amal had sat patiently through the prize giving at which I had to make a little speech about the cookbook.

'I hope it wasn't too awful,' I said, as we set out along the path towards Murchison. Amal held the torch and I was carrying the remains of my casserole.

'No, I actually enjoyed myself,' he said. 'It was quite an unusual experience.'

'Well, I'm sure you don't have many potluck suppers in Calcutta.'

It felt strange to be alone with him after the noise and confusion of the Community Centre. I felt a little awkward now that we were by ourselves, as though the darkness and the silence of the night brought us closer together. Up ahead, I could see torches flashing along the path, where it zig-zagged up the hill, a group of women going home. If I had been alone, I might have hurried to catch up with them but as it was the two of us walked slowly, as though we wanted to fall behind. The sky was very clear, even though there had been some clouds earlier in the evening.

'I wanted to apologize about the other day,' said Amal.

'That's all right,' I said, 'it wasn't your fault.'

'Well, I suppose in some ways it is my fault,' he said. 'I get so impatient with Renuka.'

'She's the one who got impatient,' I said.

'I've given up trying to persuade her to come back to Calcutta. Her mind's made up,' he said. 'I'm leaving tomorrow evening.'

'So soon?' I said.

'I've been here for two weeks,' he said. 'I really can't afford to be away from my work much longer.'

'I'm sorry your visit has been so unpleasant,' I said.

183

'I knew it wasn't going to be easy,' he said. 'My sister is a complicated woman.'

When we reached Murchison, Tick was there to greet us and I asked Amal if he would like to come inside for a cup of coffee. He glanced at his watch.

'I should be going,' he said.

'Have some coffee,' I said. 'It's not that late.'

'All right,' he said, as I unlocked the door.

I left him to deal with Tick's ecstatic welcome and went into the kitchen to put the water on. I felt bad for Amal and knew that Renuka had given him a hard time. When I came back in, he was standing in the dining room staring at the portrait of Reverend Murchison.

'Is he a relative of yours?' he asked.

'No. He's the man who built this house,' I said. 'One of the founding fathers of our mission.'

'He looks very saintly, doesn't he?' said Amal. 'A little like an old testament prophet, except for his coat and tie.'

'I think he's kind of forbidding,' I said. 'Sometimes I feel he's watching me.'

'Keeping an eye on you?' said Amal.

'Maybe,' I said.

Amal sat down on the sofa and I sat down in a chair across from him. It was such a relief to be away from the potluck.

'You aren't annoyed with me, I hope,' said Amal.

'Why would I be annoyed?'

'Well, Renuka is your friend,' he said. 'I seem to have made a mess of things.'

'No, you haven't,' I said. 'I know you're worried about her and she has been very unreasonable.'

'Maybe I should never have come up,' he said.

'I'm glad you did,' I said.

184

'Rachel, I don't want to spoil your friendship with Renuka,' he said.

'You haven't,' I said, 'Everything will be all right. I'll go over in a day or two. We'll patch things up.'

'She's very fond of you,' he said.

'I'm fond of her,' I said.

Before I could say anything more the kettle started to whistle and I had to get up to make our coffee. In the kitchen I found my hands were shaking as I opened the tin of Nescafé and got the cups. I felt afraid of what was happening but couldn't admit it to myself, afraid that Amal might sense my uneasiness.

When I brought the coffee in, Tick was whining at the door. He wanted to be let out.

'Shall I open the door for him?' said Amal.

'I guess so. I'm a little nervous letting him out at this time of night. They say that there's a leopard on the hillside. He's taken several dogs.'

'Well then, why don't we go out with him?'

Taking our coffee we followed Tick into the yard. The evening had grown quite cold and I wished I'd put on a sweater. Tick went snuffling off around the flowerbeds. Amal and I stood at the edge of the yard. The sky was very clear, without a moon and the stars seemed so close. The hillside was very silent and we could only see a couple of lights scattered across the valley.

Just then there was a soft noise in the tree above us, a rustle of leaves. Both of us looked up.

'Maybe it's the leopard,' said Amal.

'I think it must be a flying squirrel.' I said. 'There are a lot of them up here.'

I heard it scrambling up the trunk and then the soft, chirring sound which I recognized. Putting down his coffee Amal shone his torch up into the branches. All I could see were oak leaves.

'There he is,' said Amal, finally. 'He's right there against the trunk.'

'I can't see him,' I said.

The torch beam was shining on one spot but no matter how hard I looked, all I could see was the twisted shapes of the branches. Amal reached over and put his arm around my shoulder. He waved the torch a little to see if he could make the squirrel move.

'He's in that shadow,' said Amal, whispering. 'He'll move in just a moment.'

Amal kept his arm around me, one hand resting on my shoulder. We waited like this for several minutes, both of us straining our eyes on the spot where the torch beam lit up the tree. I had put my coffee down beside his cup.

'There,' said Amal. 'See him?'

The squirrel had finally moved and I could just make out his silhouette. A second later, though, he turned his head and this time his eyes shone in the torchlight and I could see his tiny, whiskered face peering down at us. The brightness of his eyes startled me, like two gold coins. Without thinking, I put my arm around Amal's waist and he pulled me closer to his side. The squirrel looked down at us for a moment and he seemed to be as surprised by us as we had been by him. Making the chirring call once more, he scurried up the tree and disappeared. Amal switched off the torch.

It seemed very dark without the light and my eyes were still shining from the glare. Amal turned towards me, his hand sliding off my shoulder and down my back. For a second, I thought he was letting go but then I saw that he was putting down the torch. He turned to face me and very slowly we embraced. I had known it was coming but I couldn't help but be surprised. His jacket was rough against my face. My arms felt very heavy, as though I couldn't move at all, but when he kissed me, I had to reach up and catch ahold of him. Whatever

186

hesitation I might have had before was gone. His beard felt so good against my face and I could taste the bitterness of the coffee on his tongue. It was happening as if to someone else, and I felt as though I was outside myself and watching, maybe like the squirrel up there in the tree.

I drew away and glanced back at the house. There was only the light in the living room. Amal knew what I was thinking and smiled. I put my face against his jacket again and closed my eyes. I had forgotten how nice it felt, just being held. After a little while I heard a rustling in the tree again. Amal and I both looked up. Even without the torch, I could see the branches swaying at the top. Then all of a sudden, the squirrel took to the air. There was a soft whistling sound as it glided out in front of the yard and down the hill. I could see its shape in the darkness, the tail, the outstretched legs and the open wings. A few seconds later, I heard it land in the trees below us. It gave me a strange, weightless feeling in my arms and legs as if I had been the one who'd leaped and soared off into the night.

I let Amal kiss me once again. This time he leaned back against the fence and lifted me off my feet. I was afraid that the fence might break and we would both go tumbling down the hill but he held me tightly and nothing seemed to matter any more.

Later, we made love in my bedroom. I had never thought that I would be able to do this with anyone but Frank. I wanted to cry because there was something wonderful about our nakedness and the way I was surprised by his desire, how easily our bodies came together. I loved the smell of him, his hair, his breath, the way he put his hands behind my shoulders, looking down at me, so serious, the way his hair fell over his eyes and his mouth opened, the soft weight between my legs. The bed creaked and we shifted a little, awkward for a moment, but then moving once again to the rhythm of our pleasure, so easily, like a stream flowing over smooth rocks. I pushed him gently on his side and lifted myself on top of him, as if to let him rest but also because I wanted him to look at me. Pressing down, I could feel myself opening further and further inward. He was moving beneath me and his eyes were closed as if he were tossing in his sleep. 'Amal!' I said, 'Amal!' Just the sound of his name. Then swiftly, something overtook us. We were like statues that came to life, those first pulsations burning through our limbs. He struggled, but I had him pinned beneath me. He could not escape except into my body and there it was, the first shiver of love and I went with him, travelling into the night, away from the creaking bed, away from the hillside, away from the voices of those women which rang in my ears like a chorus of cicadas on a monsoon night.

CHAPTER 14

DEVILLED EGGS   **Blanche Jones**

10 hard boiled eggs   1/2 cup mayonnaise
2 tablespoons paprika   1 tablespoon curry powder
1 tablespoon dry mustard   1 tablespoon salt

Slice the eggs in half and remove the yolks. Mix the yolks with the spices and mayonnaise in a separate bowl until they are a smooth paste. Refill the egg whites with the paste. This can be done with a decorative nozzle. For garnish use coriander leaves or chopped green onions.

The last person I wanted to see that morning was Blanche Jones but she arrived before I'd even finished breakfast. I was sitting by myself in the dining room, trying not to think about the consequences of what had happened the night before. Amal had left around three in the morning and I had been unable to sleep until dawn. Around eight o'clock Bindru wakened me by dropping a saucepan in the kitchen. For a while I lay in bed, just thinking and trying to decide if the whole thing could have been a dream. There was a feeling of detachment that came over me as I closed my eyes and remembered making love to Amal, a sense of having stepped beyond my imagination.

Blanche came knocking at the window, squinting at me through the glass. I knew that it had to be something important. Blanche is one of the nurses at the hospital, a miss-sahib

189

who lives just up the hill from us. I often see her coming home in the morning after night duty, in her crisp white uniform, navy blue sweater and little peaked cap. I've never really known what to make of her, since she seems to keep to herself most of the time.

'Rachel, I'm sorry to come so early but I thought you'd want to know that your friend is in the hospital,' she said.

For a moment I didn't understand.

'Who?' I said.

'That Indian woman, Renuka Sen,' said Blanche, 'One of the coolies found her in the ravine below Kisli Lodge. She must have walked right off the path.'

'Is she badly hurt?' I said.

'Well, she may have a concussion and four of her ribs are cracked; she's also fractured her wrist. I was there when they brought her in. She looked a mess, must have lain there for a couple of hours at least before somebody discovered her.'

'Thank you for telling me,' I said. 'I'll go right over. Her brother should be at Erinfell.'

'We sent a note up there around six this morning. He got to the hospital just as I was leaving.'

'Is she going to be all right?' I said.

'I think so. Doctor Foster was checking for internal injuries.'

Blanche has an irritating way of talking, her nasal voice like an announcer on the radio.

'Excuse me,' I said, 'I need to get dressed. I don't know how this could have happened.'

'Well, I can tell you how it happened,' said Blanche. 'Plain and simple: she was drunk. I could smell it on her when they brought her in, as if she'd bathed in alcohol. It's disgraceful.'

I didn't say anything more to Blanche but hurried into my bedroom. By the time I came out, pulling on a sweater, she had left. The thought of Renuka lying injured in the dark with nobody there to help her made me feel so terrible, as though it was all my fault. I couldn't understand how Amal hadn't known that she'd gone out. I remembered the evening, two nights before, when she had come to Murchison and told me about Amal's wife, the way she had headed off without a torch. It could have happened any number of times before, but why this evening, why did it have to happen now?

There is a short cut to the hospital from our house. Usually I take the longer route, around by the school, but today I scrambled down the path, slipping once or twice and almost falling. That would be just great, I thought, both of us in the hospital with broken bones.

When I got to the hospital, one of the older nurses, Mrs Peter was in the hall. I asked her where Renuka was and she looked at me with a frown.

'Dr Foster is with her right now,' she said. 'He's just doing her stitches. I'll call you when he's finished.'

I found Amal in the waiting room. He stood up when I came in and shook his head. There were several other people in the room, a couple of villagers and one of the teachers from the school, whom I didn't really know.

'What happened?' I said.

'Rachel, I don't know. When I got back, I assumed she was asleep. Her bedroom door was closed. The lights were off. I went to bed and the next thing I knew, Savitri was pounding on my door saying that Renuka had fallen down the hill.'

'She must have been out on a walk.'

'At two o'clock in the morning?'

'I spoke with one of the nurses, she said that Renuka was drunk.'

'Damn,' said Amal, loudly enough so that the teacher looked across at us.

'Have you seen her yet?' I said.

'They let me in for a few minutes when I first arrived. She was unconscious and looked pretty bad, her face all bruised and there's a gash across her forehead. I can't imagine how she could have banged herself up so badly.'

'I know the place she fell,' I said. 'It's quite a drop, thirty, forty feet.'

'I should have known this would happen,' said Amal. 'She's been drinking more than usual.'

'What could you have done?' I said. 'I'm as much to blame.'

'Well, thank god she's still alive.'

The hospital has strange associations for me. Both of the boys were born here and the delivery rooms are on the top floor. I also spent a week in the hospital one time when I got a bad case of viral fever several years ago. It's not a very pleasant place, sort of dingy and with a sour, antiseptic smell. It used to be the old military hospital before the missions took it over. From the outside it looks a little like a prison, with grey stone walls and tiny windows. There is a balcony which runs along the top and for some reason the roof has a spire in the centre like a kind of party hat with a cross on top. I don't know why anyone would make a hospital so dark and forbidding. There's an unhealthy feeling about the place. The waiting room hasn't changed in the twelve years that I've been here. There is a rack of Bible literature on one wall and a painting of Jesus knocking at the door. I remember bringing the boys to the hospital to get their shots. They would howl and scream. I can imagine the wards full of convalescent British soldiers, suffering from all kinds of tropical diseases.

Mrs Peter came and called us. She said that Dr Foster had just finished doing the stitches and we could go up and see Renuka if we liked. They'd moved her from the recovery room to a private ward. Amal followed me up the stairs. The silence of the building made me feel like an intruder. We found the room and without knocking I turned the doorknob quietly and went inside. There were two beds in the room but Renuka was the only patient there. Her eyes were closed and sunken and the bruise on her face made her look quite different. The stitches which the doctor had put in were just above one eye and covered by a gauze bandage. They'd had to shave some of her hair and the rest had been pinned back so that it wouldn't fall over the wound. I couldn't see the rest of her injuries, but underneath the sheets she looked so small and crumpled.

Amal and I stood beside the bed without saying anything. The room was fairly bright and outside the window I could see the rooftops of the bazaar and further off, the distant plains. There were two chairs in the room but we kept standing. Renuka's breathing was uneven, her lips swollen and discoloured. I was afraid to speak with Amal for fear of waking her. It gave me an uneasy feeling to see her like this, almost as though we were looking at her corpse and she was somewhere else, still wandering about the hillside in the dark like Margaret Proctor's ghost. I had been trying to ignore the thought that maybe Renuka had done this all on purpose. Maybe she had tried to kill herself, but it hadn't worked.

After we had been there for an hour or so and Renuka was still asleep, Amal went back up to Erinfell. He looked exhausted and I knew he blamed himself for what had happened. I was tired but somehow I couldn't leave Renuka there alone. Mrs Peter brought me some lunch on one of the hospital trays, and a pot of tea. She didn't say anything but I could tell that she disapproved of Renuka and did not like the idea of my being her friend. Mrs Peter is an Indian Christian and she has been at the hospital for years. She was there when Tim and Michael were born and used to give the boys their typhoid/cholera shots. When they cried she would tell them that this was the way they howled when they were babies. She is a good nurse, quick and efficient, but always a little severe.

I didn't eat much lunch but as I was drinking a second cup of tea, I heard Renuka make a soft crying sound. When I got up from the chair, she was moving her head and her breathing had changed. One of her hands had slipped from beneath the sheets and when I touched it, she looked at me, her eyes dazed and only half open. She said my name very softly.

'You'll be all right,' I said.

'I fell,' she said, her face tightening.

'Don't try to talk,' I said.

'It was so dark. I tried to shout for help,' she said, her voice slurred, each word an effort.

'You're okay. You're in the hospital now.'

'I feel like such a fool,' she said.

'Don't,' I said.

'Amal?' she said.

'He was here a little while ago. He had to go up to Erinfell. He'll be back.'

She pulled her hand from mine and touched her face, on the side where it was bruised. Afterwards, I wished I'd had a camera just to show her how dreadful she looked, the cut above her eye, the whole left side of her face swollen black and blue. Even her hair seemed to have lost its lustre. Three days later, when I finally got her to sit up and look in a mirror, the swelling had gone down completely and even the bruise didn't look as bad. She wouldn't believe me when I told her how awful she'd looked.

Amal returned about an hour later. He had brought some clothes for Renuka, her nightgown and some other things which he had packed into an overnight bag. By that time, the pain in her ribs had become worse and she couldn't speak without crying out. Amal sent one of the nurses to call Dr Foster. He came after a few minutes and said that he had taped her chest and it would hurt for several weeks but there was nothing to worry about. They would give her a pain-killer in an hour or two so that she could sleep. Dr Foster is a pleasant man and very easy-going. Unlike the nurses he didn't seem to pass judgement on Renuka for what she'd done. He said that she'd be up and around in a couple of days and even teased her a little about her midnight walk.

I decided to spend the night at the hospital, since there was an extra bed in Renuka's room. The boys would not be back from their hike until the following day. Renuka tried to shake her head when I told her what I was doing, but there was no way she could stop me. While Amal stayed with her, I walked back up to Murchison and got my toothbrush and a change of clothes. Mrs Peter had gone off duty by the time I returned and one of the younger nurses brought me an extra pillow.

With the pain-killer Renuka was able to sleep for several hours and I also got a chance to lie down. By then I was so tired, I fell asleep before I'd even shut my eyes. Later in the night, Renuka got restless and woke me up to get her some water.

'I wouldn't mind a real drink,' she said, as I put one hand behind her head to raise her up.

'That's what got you into all this trouble.'

She gave a weak smile.

'What time is it?' she said.

'Almost midnight.'

'Thank you for staying with me.'

I kissed her hand.

'You must think I'm an idiot,' she said.

I shook my head. She had to catch her breath between each word.

'What were you doing, walking around the hillside at two o'clock in the morning?' I said.

Renuka rolled her eyes and I almost wished I hadn't asked her.

'I was looking for Amal,' she said. 'I thought he'd lost his way, coming home in the dark.'

'You'd been drinking,' I said.

'Was he with you?' she said.

'Yes,' I said.

Renuka closed her eyes.

'How many bones have I broken?' she said.

'Four ribs,' I said. 'And you've fractured your wrist.'

'What about my head?' she said.

'It's just a cut,' I said.

'I didn't crack my skull?'

'No, you were lucky,' I said.

'Did Amal make love to you?' she said.

I nodded.

'Rachel. Rachel.' She tried to laugh but it made her gasp with pain.

'You shouldn't be talking,' I said.

'I wasn't really jealous,' said Renuka, after she had caught her breath. 'Only a little.'

'You shouldn't be,' I said.

'I know,' she said. 'It's just the way I am.'

'It doesn't matter,' I said and kissed her hand. 'I love you, Renuka.'

She was quiet for a while. I could see that she was crying, the tears slipping down her bruised cheeks and falling on the pillow.

'Can you call the nurse?' she said. 'Ask her if she'll give me another injection, so that I can sleep.'

Sunday afternoon the boys came back from their hike with all sorts of stories about seeing a bear near their tent and how Michael had almost been swept away while they were crossing a stream. I took them to see Renuka and even though she was still in a lot of pain, I think it cheered her up to hear about their adventures. Renuka let them sign their names on her cast and told them that this should be a lesson to them when they went climbing down the khud.

Amal had postponed his departure for a few days, until Renuka was ready to come home. He and I made love once more at Erinfell, before he left. I told the boys that I was going to visit Renuka at the hospital that night. I felt bad lying to them but I knew that I would probably never see Amal again.

'Are you going to tell your husband?' he said.

'What about?' I said.

'About me,' he said.

'I haven't really made up my mind,' I said.

'He doesn't have to know,' said Amal.

'I told Renuka,' I said.

'Was she angry?'

It made me laugh, the way he asked. 'No, I don't think so,' I said.

'I never know how she'll react.'

'Are you really leaving tomorrow?' I said.

He nodded. 'I've got to get back to work. We have a big campaign coming up,' he said. 'It's for lemon squash, a new brand that's coming onto the market.'

'Is it any good?' I said.

'To tell you the truth,' he said, 'I've never tasted it. Do you remember that old tune, "Joshua, Joshua, sweeter than lemon squash you are?"'

'No,' I said, 'I've never heard it.'

'I think it's from an old Cliff Richard song,' said Amal. 'We're changing it around a bit. The company's name is Benton, Joshua, and Bannerjee and we're going to have a jingle on the radio, "Joshua, Joshua the sweetest of lemon squash you are."'

'That's very clever,' I said.

'No it isn't,' he said, 'but now you know the sort of important things I do in my life, thinking up jingles about lemon squash.'

197

'Why don't you advertise it in our cookbook?' I said. 'We're going to have some ads at the back to help cover our printing costs.'

'Of course,' he said. 'We'll take a full page.'

'That costs four hundred rupees.'

'No problem,' said Amal. 'I'll send you a cheque and a copy of the ad when I get to Calcutta.'

The next day we were able to get a dandie to take Renuka home from the hospital. She kept insisting that she could walk but her ribs were still hurting pretty badly and it would be another week at least before she was really up and around again.

Amal left the same evening. He had a booking on the train and caught a taxi down the hill at about five o'clock. I had been worried about saying goodbye to him but with Renuka there it was easier. We kissed each other on the cheek. After he had left, I sat with Renuka for a while in her living room.

'Are you sad to see him leave?' she said.

'A little,' I said. 'But I think it's better this way.'

'Rachel, you're such a practical person,' she said. 'So level-headed and unemotional.'

'That's hardly true,' I said.

'It is,' she said. 'You're not at all like me, getting so irrational and upset.'

'It doesn't matter.'

'I really don't know what you saw in him,' she said. 'My brother's such a fool.'

'I don't think you realize how much he cares about you,' I said. 'He was very worried.'

'Hah!' said Renuka. 'That's just the way he talks.'

'No,' I said. 'He really wants you to go back to Calcutta.'

'He wants me to keep house for him, that's all,' said Renuka.

198

'I doubt if that's the reason,' I said. 'Amal has a lot of respect for you and he doesn't like to see you wasting away up here.'

'So, you agree with him?' she said. 'You think I should go back to Calcutta?'

'I don't want to see you leave, Renuka. But I know that I'm not going to stay here for the rest of my life. You can't just go on living by yourself.'

'Why not?'

'You're not that kind of person,' I said. 'You shouldn't be hiding up here like this.'

'I'm not hiding,' she said.

'I think you are, you're hiding from yourself.'

'Since when have you become a psychologist?' she said.

'I'm not,' I said, 'but I am your friend. Tell me why you don't want to go back.'

Renuka closed her eyes. She had her cast cradled in her lap, holding it with her other hand.

'Bad memories,' she said.

'You mean Amal's wife?' I said.

'No, nothing to do with that,' said Renuka. 'I had a very close friend in Calcutta, a woman named Aruna Pande. She was quite a bit younger than me, a college girl. I had just published a book of poems and she came to the house one day and introduced herself. Aruna was also a poet and she wrote some of the most moving, lyrical verses I've ever read. I recommended her work to several publishers and her poems appeared in one or two influential magazines. She became quite popular in literary circles and people began to discuss her writing very seriously. She had such a natural talent. I was proud of her, not just because she was my protegé but because she was my friend. Aruna's family came from Patna and she was all alone in Calcutta, trying to get her degree in English literature. She was staying at a women's hostel, a miserable little place in an unpleasant part of the city. I invited her to come and live with

199

me and I gave her a room of her own, adjoining mine, where she could sleep and work.

'Aruna was very quiet, shy as a kitten and sometimes I would go into her room and she would be bent over her desk, scribbling away at a sheet of paper, so intent on what she was writing that she didn't even know that I was watching her.

'I used to take her to parties, the usual cocktail circuit, a lot of pompous old windbags and epileptic young journalists who threw their arms about when they talked. She seemed so frightened in the midst of all these voluble fools. I felt protective towards her. Aruna was so sensitive, so easily upset. One time she even asked me if I would publish a poem which she had written under my name because she thought it might be controversial. Aruna was terrified of criticism and there was something so fragile about her that made me want to shield her from everyone.

'She stayed with me for almost a year and it was like having a child in the house. I loved her very much and sometimes when she was depressed, she would come to me and put her head in my lap and cry. She used to get nightmares and I would wake up and find her standing by my bed, trembling and afraid. After a while I let her sleep with me so that she wouldn't be alone. We would lie together and I would play with her hair and tell her about my schooldays in Darjeeling, the nuns, the orchids in the trees, the mist over the tea gardens. She had never been up to the mountains and had no idea what it was like.

'One night, as we were lying there, I started to make love to her. It was almost as if it happened by accident. We had gone to see a film and maybe something in the story had aroused me. It was summer and both of us were wearing very little. There was a ceiling fan but the air was hot and humid. My hands moved over her breasts and down her legs. Aruna didn't seem to mind and for a while I thought she'd gone to sleep, she lay so still. I kissed her shoulders and then her face. Even though

200

it was dark, I could see her eyes were open. She let me take her in my arms. I asked her if she was frightened but she shook her head. She took my hand and touched herself, as if to show me how.'

Renuka stopped and looked at me.

'Are you shocked?' she said.

'No,' I said.

'You don't find it disgusting?'

'Go on. What happened after that?' I said.

Renuka laughed.

'What do you mean, what happened?' she said. 'Silly Rachel, can't you guess? Or do I have to spell it out for you?'

'No, I can guess,' I said, also laughing. 'I meant, what happened to Aruna? Did she leave?'

'Not for a while,' said Renuka, her voice a little softer. 'But eventually. Her parents called her back to Patna. They married her off to some civil servant.'

'But didn't she object?' I said.

'Not really,' said Renuka. 'That was one of the peculiar things about Aruna. She was quite content to let her family run her life. I had no choice. I had no hold on her. I had to let her go.'

'But wasn't she in love with you?' I said.

Renuka shook her head.

'No, I don't think so, at least not in a way that you or I would understand. For her it was a game,' said Renuka.

'And what was it for you?' I said.

'Like nothing I had ever known,' said Renuka. 'A kind of emptiness which only she could fill. When Aruna left, I felt so miserable. I couldn't stand being in that room without her or sleeping in that bed. I began to hate Calcutta, all the places we had been together, the bazaars, the coffee shops, the theatres, the book stores, the hotel lobbies, everything seemed so empty. Even in the middle of the day when there were crowds

201

around me, I always felt as if there was nobody, nobody beside me, nobody to hold my hand, nobody to whisper in my ear.'

'But then why did you come up here,' I said, 'where you'd really be alone?'

'Because I needed to be away from everything that reminded me of her,' she said.

Renuka had turned her face aside, staring into the shadows. As I got up, she didn't move. I went across and put my arms around her. She wasn't crying but there was a look on her face that frightened me, a sad expression which made her seem so cold and distant.

'Now, go,' she said. 'Go home. I've told you everything.'

CHAPTER 15

RHODODENDRON JELLY   **Rachel Manton**

2 lbs Rhododendron petals
4 cups Sugar
3 Lemons
1 packet Surejell

To prepare the rhododendron petals, remove the white stamens carefully and wash the petals in a large basin. Make sure that all the stamens have been removed, otherwise they give a bitter flavor to the jelly. Boil the petals in two quarts of water for thirty minutes. Strain the juice through a fine sieve and add the Sugar, Lemon juice and Surejell. Simmer for fifteen minutes, stirring constantly and then allow to cool before bottling. Quantity: 8 medium sized bottles of jelly.

I hardly ever use the cookbook any more but I enjoy flipping through the recipes to remind myself of the hillside. I remember the rhododendrons would start to bloom in March, just after I came up to put the boys in school. Those dull, green trees would suddenly blossom with huge bouquets of red. The Himalayan rhododendrons are different to the ones we have in our yard in Minneapolis, these pale lavender flowers that grow on bushes beneath my kitchen window. Those were full-grown trees and the blossoms were a brilliant, scarlet red. It looked as though someone had gone all over the hillside and tied christmas decorations on every branch.

The boys would go out with pillowcases and collect the flowers for me every spring and I would faithfully sit and pick out the white stamens, wondering if it was really worth the trouble. It would take so many flowers to make a few jars of jelly. I read somewhere that the rhododendrons in America are poisonous and when I told one of the women in our church that we used to make them into jelly, she looked at me as if she didn't believe what I was saying. They think I'm a little peculiar anyway, having been a missionary. The boys didn't really like rhododendron jelly very much but they enjoyed picking the flowers, especially if I offered them two rupees a pound. Tim and Michael used to eat the flowers just plain and made me try them once. They had a sour, fruity taste, a little like Roselle, which I used to grow in our garden in Ranchi.

There are days when I can see the rhododendron trees so clearly in my mind, those splashes of colour on cold, grey afternoons. They were the first spring flowers and came out even before the apricot blossoms. I remember there were a lot of rhododendron trees near the graveyard on the north side of the hill. One day I went up there for a walk and found that somebody had put a blossom on every gravestone. They looked like splashes of blood.

Renuka had a rhododendron tree just below her house. One time she brought an enormous armload of flowers over to Murchison and we couldn't find a vase big enough to hold them all. Finally, I got one of the tin buckets from the bathroom and we put the flowers in there. It didn't make a very elegant vase but the rhododendrons were so beautiful themselves that it didn't really matter. I always thought that the flowers should have a scent but they were odourless and it was only when I put them on to boil that they gave off a faint perfume. The jelly has a delicate flavour and a clear red colour. I gave Renuka a jar from the first batch I made and she was delighted. She told me that I should go into business with her and we could start selling the stuff in stores. Renuka always had some scheme but she seemed to take this one very seriously and started thinking of a name and label for the bottles: 'Rachel and Renuka's Rhododendron Preserves'. I think I finally convinced her that it wouldn't work when she came over and helped me pick stamens after the boys had gathered twenty pillowcases full. Even at a hundred rupees a bottle it wouldn't have been worth the trouble. In the end, Renuka made some rhododendron wine but didn't have the patience to let it age. I had a taste and it was pretty awful. Renuka said the wine had a powerful kick but I never took more than a tiny glass.

I think I miss her most of all, the way she talked, her gestures, her language, the way she played with her hair, teasing it between her fingers, the way her eyes moved and flashed like sapphires, her laughter and her stories. She had a way of startling me with the smallest things. Just when I thought I knew her, she would behave in the most unexpected way. Somehow I didn't care. It didn't matter that she would make up the most outrageous stories about herself, imaginary adventures which only I would believe. Sometimes I thought that she should have written novels instead of poems, but on paper her stories wouldn't have made any sense at all. They were like scenes from a dream that seemed so real but couldn't possibly be true.

Renuka and I still keep in touch, though neither of us is very good at letter writing. This Christmas I sent her some pictures of the boys and she wrote back and said she wouldn't have recognized them if I hadn't written their names on the back of the photographs. She is still living in her family home, though she and Amal have rented out the upper floor, since there are just the two of them. Her letter was longer than usual and I got a feeling that she missed being at Erinfell even though her life seemed very busy. She had just published a new book of poems, some of which she'd written on the hillside. Renuka promised to send me the English translations when she had them ready. She complained about Calcutta and said that it was getting worse and worse each day, the smoke and stench, the traffic and the overcrowding but at the same time she seemed to be enjoying herself and mentioned several friends, including an artist who had done her portrait. She said that she would have the painting photographed and send me a copy, though it probably wouldn't look as nice as the original, which was a little abstract. She also mentioned that Amal sent his greetings.

I still remember how surprised I was the morning after she told me about Aruna, when I walked over to Erinfell and found Renuka sitting on the verandah, surrounded by boxes and trunks. Savitri was helping her to pack and Renuka was giving instructions, waving her plaster arm about.

'Rachel!' she shouted, when she saw me at the gate. 'Come here! I want you to take whatever you want.'

She pointed to the piles of her belongings which were scattered around the verandah, her statues and paintings, all of the odds and ends from her living room shelves.

'What's going on?' I said.

'I've changed my mind,' she said. 'Since you don't seem to want me here, I've decided there isn't any reason to stay.'

'You're going back to Calcutta,' I said.

'Yes, I'm going to give my brother a surprise,' said Renuka. 'Now don't just stand there. I need your help. Maybe you could make a list of all these things. With my bloody arm, I can't write at all.'

'But what about Savitri?' I said. It was the first thing that came into my mind.

'Oh, she's going with me,' said Renuka. 'It was her idea. She's never seen a city before.'

206

I felt suddenly empty and afraid, as if I hadn't really wanted this to happen, even though I'd told Renuka that she should go back home. Seeing the half-filled trunks, the stacks of books, I couldn't help but feel it was my fault that Renuka was leaving. And yet, at the same time there was a sense of relief, as if I was waking out of a disturbing dream, a kind of lingering sadness.

Saying goodbye to Renuka was one of the hardest things I've ever done. It took her a week and a half to pack up everything and ship it off and she wanted to wait until her stitches were taken out before she set off for Calcutta. She spent the last two nights with us at Murchison and I set up a bed for her in the extra room. She seemed excited to be going and we stayed up late, talking about all the things she planned to do. I didn't really feel so bad about saying goodbye until the day that she was going and then I started getting weepy. She kept saying that she would come back and visit me or maybe I could go and stay with her in Calcutta. But that was just to make us feel a little better.

I walked down to the bazaar with her. We were a little late and I was worried that Renuka would miss her train, but she didn't seem too bothered. The coolies had gone ahead and we told them to load the luggage into a taxi. When we got to the clocktower, I decided not to go any further and said that I was turning back. She looked at me and smiled as if she knew that I didn't have the courage to go any further. We hugged each other so hard I was worried that I might hurt her ribs. Everyone in the bazaar was looking at us, as if the two of us were crazy. She whispered something in my ear about writing letters. After I let go of her, she turned deliberately away and set off down the road, the cast on her arm swinging at her side and her head thrown back as though she was fighting the urge to turn around. I watched her until she disappeared into the crowd of tourists and villagers along the mall.

*

It's been eight years since I left the hillside, eight years since the cookbook was finally finished and I told Frank that it was time for us to leave. I was surprised how easily he agreed and maybe I'd misjudged him all those years. He can be very reasonable sometimes. I think Frank knew that he had come to the point where he would have to turn over the mental home to someone else or stay there for the rest of his life. As it turned out, there was a young Indian psychologist who was perfect for the job. He had worked in Bombay for several years and Frank seemed to have a lot of confidence in him. The boys weren't so happy about going back to America, though the thought of television and things like that appealed to them. It took us about six months to close up everything and ship our luggage. I had to sell a lot of our things to the kabadiwallahs, the junk dealers who came around the hillside collecting things from missionaries who were leaving.

Bindru retired and went back to his village. I had finally talked him into getting his cataracts operated on and once he could see again, he seemed more cheerful and optimistic. We helped him clear his debts and I think he actually looked forward to going home to his wife and children.

Tick died a short while after Renuka left. He was sick for several weeks even though he kept on chasing monkeys until the end. One day I found him lying dead in the flowerbeds behind the house. It must have been his heart. We buried him down in the ravine below Murchison. I didn't think I would cry because of that stupid dog, all the times I'd shouted at him or rolled up a newspaper and threatened to club him over the head. The boys were in tears for several days but they got over it and Michael said, 'at least he didn't get eaten by a leopard.'

We had to go down to Ranchi and spent another month packing up the rest of our things. The farewells there were easier for me though Frank got quite emotional when he was saying goodbye to the staff and patients. They had a little ceremony before we left and garlanded us with marigolds. It was the middle of June by the time we finally took the train to Delhi and flew home. It had been so many years since I had been on the plains in summer and I was surprised how I didn't mind the heat that much. In the middle of the day it was oppressive and we did most of our packing after dark but when the electricity was on and the fans were turned up, it wasn't all that bad. Frank said it was a mild summer.

Once we had made up our minds to go back to America, Frank and I talked about different places we might go. I didn't want to live in Chicago and there wasn't much reason to go back, though Frank has relatives in Evanston. Minneapolis had always seemed like a nice place to live and it is only forty miles from Hopkins, where my mother lives. Frank wrinkled up his nose when I mentioned it at first. He has this thing about Minnesota, as though it's the most boring place in the world, but in the end I convinced him that he should look around in the Minneapolis/St Paul area for a job. He wrote ahead and when we got there, he visited a couple of state institutions and one or two private clinics. I had been worried that Frank would have trouble finding work but he got several offers the first month we were there and he finally accepted a job in a private clinic which did a lot of work amongst the poorer people. Living in India you forget that there are poor people in America, especially in Minnesota.

I can't believe how easily our lives have changed. We bought a house in a suburb about half an hour's drive from the clinic where Frank works. There is a good public school just down the road from us. Tim and Michael had some trouble adjusting but after the first semester they'd made some friends and Tim was going steady with a much nicer girl than Susan Carson. For a while I just enjoyed being by myself at home, without any servants or boxwallahs coming to the door. We found a church which we liked nearby and I even started driving again, which is something I had never done in India. Tim and I took our driving test on the same day and we were both so nervous I was sure that we were going to fail. There are times when I am standing in the kitchen and it strikes me, how far away the hillside is. We brought a lot of our things with us from India, the rosewood elephants which stood on the mantlepiece at Murchison and a copper tray which I have hung in the dining room of our new house. Before she left, Renuka gave me a miniature painting from her wall, one that I had always admired, of a Rajput princess having her hair combed by a maidservant and in the background, a sandstone fortress on a hill. I didn't want to accept it when she gave it to me but Renuka had insisted. I hung the miniature in the living room for a while but then I moved it into our bedroom on the wall above my dressing table where I could see it every morning when I woke up.

It's nice to be a family once again, though Tim is going to college now and living in a dormitory. Michael is in his senior year of high school. All of us miss India a lot but we have come together in a way that would never have been possible with Frank in Ranchi and the boys and I on the hillside. It's been especially good for Frank. I used to worry about him quite a lot. He didn't look well at all and after we came back to the States, I made him go to a doctor and have a check up. Frank has always hated going to a doctor, even though he is one himself. The doctors advised him to get more exercise. He didn't need to lose any weight but he was out of shape. I didn't think he would take it very seriously but he has and now he goes for a run every morning before he leaves for work.

I've found he's more relaxed, more talkative and we do a lot of things together that we would never have done in India. There's a theatre in the shopping mall near our house and we try to see a movie once a month. It's not like the old Odeon with its tattered velvet curtains and box seats and there isn't an old woman sitting outside on the pavement selling peanuts. The theatre is kind of small and doesn't have much character but I enjoy it anyway and I hold Frank's hand. A couple of the movies we've seen have been pretty risqué. The first time the actors started taking off their clothes, I felt Frank squirm. They didn't used to have all of that stuff in the movies when we were young, maybe a good long kiss and lots of tight sweaters, but not the sort of nudity they show you nowadays and certainly not the scenes of people making love. It was a shock at first but we can laugh about it now. I guess that comes from not being missionaries any more.

Frank doesn't know about Amal. I've never told him and I don't think I ever will. If I was going to confess to him, I would have done it long ago; besides, I don't really feel I need to give a confession. I still love Frank. I am his wife and if I've been unfaithful to him then it was just for a day or two and what's that against twenty-five years. We celebrated our anniversary the other day and he took me out to dinner at a fancy restaurant downtown where they have these fountains in the middle of the room and a revolving chandelier. It was nice and we each had a glass of wine. That's another thing that's changed. I remember how Renuka used to have to persuade me to have a drink and I never really liked the stuff, but I have acquired a taste for red wine, though I'll never be a connoisseur and more than one glass makes me silly.

I used to think that if you kept a secret for too long it would begin to rot inside of you. Maybe I felt that way because Frank is a psychiatrist and they're supposed to get all those secrets out of you and lay them on the table, like some sort of psychological dissection. Anyway, I did tell Renuka, and maybe that was enough, but I really don't feel guilty any more.

Whenever I think of Amal and making love to him it seems like something which I can hold onto without ever telling

Frank. If I felt dishonest or ashamed, I might have told him, but it's really something all my own, a kind of personal memory which doesn't have to be revealed. For a while I thought that I would change because of it but that doesn't have to happen, unless there's something else which makes you change. Maybe Renuka was right about me being practical. I know that what I did might be called a sin but I can't look at it like that. There wasn't anything immoral about it. I'm not interested in going out and finding other men. It wasn't that kind of an affair and I know that I don't need to make excuses.

The best part of coming back to Minneapolis was being able to see my mother more often and talking to her on the phone. She is living in an apartment now in Hopkins. The farm was finally sold, which was sad. I went out there with her just after all the papers had been signed, for one last visit. It looked so much the same, though the barn didn't seem quite as large as it used to be when I was a girl and the trees along the driveway were much taller. I had been back each furlough but this time it was different. My mother and I walked down to the pond. The sauna was still there, though nobody had used it for years. We opened it up and there was still the faint smell of cedar. I could remember the knots in the boards from when I was a girl and we played hide and seek down there. When I told my mother how I remembered the story about her family running naked out into the snow and plunging through the ice she looked at me suspiciously.

'We'd never have done a thing like that,' she said.

'But you told me.'

My mother peered inside the sauna once again, as if to remind herself. She shook her head.

'Rachel,' she said, 'I can't imagine how such a thing was possible.'

'But I remember,' I said, insistently. 'You told me one day, right after the sauna was built, grandpa and grandma and you and uncle Swen and some of the others all came down and tried it out for the first time and once you had a good steam worked up and it was so hot you couldn't bear it any more, all of you ran down to the pond and jumped through the ice.'

Mother frowned at me and then I saw the mischief in her eyes and knew I hadn't made it up. She didn't say anything and closed the door of the sauna, fumbling with the latch.

'Some things are best forgotten,' she said.

I suppose that's true. I don't want to make it sound as though it was easy coming back. We had our difficult times as well. Michael went through a moody stage which surprised me. He had always been so cheerful and energetic as a younger boy, always the one who went outdoors even if it was raining. Tim was more likely to get upset with things. Michael had a way of letting everything slide off his back. But during his freshman year of highschool he had problems with some of his classmates and for a while Frank and I were worried that he was getting involved with a rougher crowd than we would like. He grew away from us for several years and sometimes he would come home and go straight upstairs without saying anything, turn up his music and lock the door. I knew it was a stage that he was going through but it also worried me because he looked unhappy. I tried to talk with him about it but he would get impatient and annoyed with my questions.

Frank has always been reluctant to try and talk things through with me or with the boys. I think he doesn't like to take on the role of a psychiatrist at home. I know there is a difference between counselling a stranger and trying to solve a problem within your own family. Finally, though, I couldn't stand it any more and I told Frank that he would have to confront Michael and talk with him, not as a psychiatrist but as a father.

I should have known it wouldn't work but that night Frank went up to Michael's room and I heard the music blaring for a while. I figured that if he switched it off then maybe they would get a chance to talk. But the volume stayed the same and half an hour later Frank came out, holding his ears and shaking his head. He said that Michael just sat and stared at the floor while he tried to ask him what was wrong. I had to laugh at Frank the way he looked so helpless, as though all of his years of experience as a counsellor and confidante had come to nothing.

We never really found out what was troubling Michael but as soon as he got into his sophomore year everything seemed to turn around again. I knew I shouldn't have worried about him. It was just a phase that he was going through. The other day I asked him why he'd tried to shut us out. Michael looked a little sheepish, as though he wished I hadn't brought it up.

'It wasn't anything serious,' he said.

'Well, it sure seemed serious to me,' I said. 'You didn't talk to me for weeks.'

He grinned and rubbed his nose.

'I don't know. It's no big deal,' he said. 'I was maybe just homesick, that was all.'

'For the hillside?' I said.

He nodded. 'But that's okay. I'm over it now.'

'I miss the hillside too,' I said.

'It wasn't all that great,' he said, shrugging to show me that it didn't bother him any more.

'Well, there's no reason why you shouldn't feel homesick, Michael,' I said.

'Remember all those stupid recipes?' he said.

'Oh, come on, they weren't that bad,' I said.

'What about Mrs Turner's cornflake casserole?'

'You still remember that,' I said.

'Or that guava pudding you made us eat. It looked like dog poop.'

'Michael!' I said, but I didn't really mind, because I remembered how awful some of the recipes had been.

I am glad that we can laugh about those things because if we couldn't I would be afraid that there was something really wrong with us.

'I bet you miss Renuka,' said Michael.

'I do,' I said.

'She was such a crazy woman,' he said.

'Crazy?' I said.

'I remember one time she told me how she shot a man-eating tiger. She told me all about it, how it had killed a villager and she had to sit up in this tree over the corpse and the stink was awful and the body was half eaten. It was sick, the way she told me. Anyway the tiger came around and started chewing on his leg and she shone her torch down at it and shot it between the eyes. I believed her until she told me that the tiger started to climb the tree to eat her even though she'd blown its brains away.'

'When did she tell you that?' I said.

'I forget,' he said. 'I just remember the story and knowing that she was making it up.'

'She did tell a lot of stories,' I said. 'You're right, definitely a crazy lady.'